Puffin Books

THE END

compiled by Richard Stanley

The ultimate horror, the final extremity, the absolute and bitter end has finally been reached. Richard Stanley, instigator of *The Crack-a-Joke Book*, has produced a new monster, aided and abetted by little monsters from all over the world. Scraped up from below the bottom of the bad jokes barrel, this new collection could get no worse!

Perhaps it will fill a need – perhaps you do want to die laughing, drive your loved ones to desperation, or condemn your friends to the horrors of suffocation by giggles. All we can say is that as Fungus the Bogeyman recommends this book – YOU HAVE BEEN WARNED!

THE END

compiled by Richard Stanley

with a Foreword by
Fungus the Bogeyman

pictures by Mahood

PUFFIN BOOKS

For Giles and Matthew

Puffin Books, Penguin Books Ltd, Harmondsworth, Middlesex, England
Penguin Books, 625 Madison Avenue, New York, New York 10022, U.S.A.
Penguin Books Australia Ltd, Ringwood, Victoria, Australia
Penguin Books Canada Ltd, 2801 John Street, Markham, Ontario, Canada L3R 1B4
Penguin Books (N.Z.) Ltd, 182–190 Wairau Road, Auckland 10, New Zealand

Published in Puffin Books 1980
Reprinted 1980 (twice), 1981 (twice)
Published simultaneously in hardback by Kestrel Books 1980

Made and printed in Great Britain by
Richard Clay (The Chaucer Press) Ltd,
Bungay, Suffolk
Set in Monotype Ehrhardt

Acknowledgements

A million thanks to all those who dare admit to having had a hand in this collection: children from all over the world, who sent in their best worst jokes, and these special people who made the book possible:

Sue Bark

Raymond Briggs   Mark Kasprowicz
Colin Bunyan   John Leonard
Martin Campbell   Janice Long
Ian Collington   Timmy Mallett
Janet Crumbie   Roger Matthews
Ed Doolan   David Ryder
Nigel Dyson   John Skrine
Peter Fairhead   John Sparrow
June Harben   Petra Stanley
Sam and Joe Horowitz   Melanie Steiner

George Thaw

Also thanks to:

Young Observer
Radio One *Playground*   Radio Four *You and Yours*

Puffin Post   Metoy Toys

BRMB Birmingham   Radio Medway
Radio Birmingham   Radio Merseyside
Radio Blackburn   Radio Newcastle
Radio Brighton   Radio Nottingham
Radio Carlisle   Radio Orwell
Radio Cleveland   Radio Oxford
Radio Derby   Radio Sheffield
Radio Leeds   Radio Solent
Radio Leicester   Thames Valley Radio
          Radio Trent

Contents

A Letter from Fungus the Bogeyman

Drear Drycleaner Reader,

This vile book which you are already reading has been stinkingly popular in Bogeydom. The jokes are so rotten, so wet and so dull that readers instantly fall asleep. Some of the jokes are so old they are decayed and smelly. If you put your nose close to the joke you can actually smell it. Try this for yourself; but be careful. Some jokes are so rotten they may break away and be sniffed up your nose.

This happened several times to our editor, Richard Stanley, and it made his huge task even more boring.

Bogeys do not laugh very much. In fact, we almost never laugh at all. We are a solemn race. Bogeys also enjoy being bored. We go to boring concerts of silent music, we attend boring inaudible lectures, and we watch boring whispered plays. But, above all, we enjoy boring books.

Perhaps this explains why this appalling book is so beloved in Bogeydom. There is nothing whatsoever funny in it. Consequently, Bogeys do not have to exert themselves even *trying* to laugh. They can solemnly stare at the smelly pages and do nothing except sniff the rotten jokes and turn the decaying leaves.

The Bogey edition was printed in Bogeydom, of course. Surface presses were useless as they were far too hot and dry. The rotten wet jokes blocked up the machinery in no time at all.

Now, we know that you Drycleaners like your books to have dry non-sticky pages; so these pages have been specially sprayed, at enormous expense, to prevent the rotten, slimy, decaying putrescent jokes from composting the paper into one wet soggy, oozing lump like the Bogey edition.

Mmmmm! The Bogey edition is almost edible.

You will also be thrilled to learn that this book is so boring it is now Bottom of the Bottom Ten in Bogeydom. It is also in The Bogginness Book of Records as the dullest book ever known. Not one single Bogey has even smiled slightly at the jokes. This is a record for a joke book, even in Bogeydom.

I am told you Drycleaners actually *like* to laugh, and that you make a loud and painful noise with your horrible hot pink mouths when you do so.

Why do you do it? What is the point? It must be very tiring. Why not save your energy for sleep?

Read this book. It will not tire you at all. There is nothing funny in it. It is a real loser.

I hope it makes you sleep. It did me.

Boibye,
Yours Filthfully,

Fungus
Your Smelly Friend of The Night

Unspeakable Eatables

'Waiter, there's a fly in my soup.'
'That's all right, sir, he won't drink much.'

Sign in a restaurant:
> *Our tongue sandwiches speak for themselves.*

A gentleman dining at Crewe
Found quite a large mouse in his stew.
Said the waiter: 'Don't shout
And wave it about
Or the rest will be wanting one too.'

'Waiter, waiter, this stew isn't fit for a pig.'
'Sir, would you like me to take it away and bring you
some that is?'

'Waiter, there's a dead fly in my wine.'
'Well, you did ask for something with a little body in it.'

'Waiter, waiter, this soup tastes funny.'
'Then why aren't you laughing?'

'Waiter, there's a funny film on this soup.'
'What do you expect for 15p – *Star Wars*?'

WAITER: 'We have almost everything on the menu, sir.'
DINER: 'So I see. Will you kindly bring me a clean one?'

DINER: 'This restaurant must have very clean kitchens.'
WAITER: 'Thank you, sir, but how can you tell?'
DINER: 'Everything tastes of soap.'

'Waiter, call the manager. I can't eat this stew.'
'He wouldn't eat it either, sir.'

'Waiter, these beefburgers taste like polystyrene tiles!'
'Yes sir, that's why we charge ceiling prices.'

DINER: 'Is there soup on the menu?'
WAITER: 'No, sir, I wiped it off.'

CUSTOMER: 'Waiter, waiter, there's a dead fly in my soup.'
WAITER (*sobbing*): 'And he was so young.'

British Rail have stopped using menus in their restaurants on trains – now you just look at the tablecloth and guess.

'Waiter, your thumb is in my soup.'
'That's okay, sir, it's not hot.'

Which hand do you stir your tea with?
You don't stir it with your hand, you stir it with a spoon.

'Waiter, why have you got your thumb on my steak?'
'Well, sir, I don't want to drop it on the floor again, do I?'

'Waiter, waiter, what's this insect doing in my soup?
'Trying to get out.'

'Waiter, I'm in a hurry, will the pancake be long?'
'No, sir, it will be round.'

What's sweet, has custard and is bad tempered?
Apple grumble.

What kind of meringues come back to you?
Boomerangs.

What bean is good at hide and seek?
A soya bean.

Why did the banana go out with the prune?
He couldn't find a date.

Why did the boy put a loaf of bread in his comic?
Because he liked crummy jokes.

What flies and wobbles at the same time?
A jellycopter.

When does an astronaut have his mid-day meal?
At launch time.

Why can't you starve in the desert?
  Because of the sandwich is there.

JESS: 'Name me three kinds of nuts.'
TESS: 'Peanuts, walnuts and forget-me-nuts.'

What cheese is made backwards?
  Edam.

What nut grows on the wall?
  A walnut.

What sugar sings?
  Icing sugar.

Horrible sandwich fillings?
Custard and sand
Toothpaste and gravel
Raw liver and clay
Sawdust and candle grease
Mousetails and mustard pickle
Ashes and ice-cream
Hamster bedding and vegetable oil
Nut shells and ink
Mouldy leaves and rats' ears
Chalk dust and tree sap
Squashed worms and washing-up liquid
Dog food and bird seed
Mushy banana and cement

Recipe for crispy maggots in chocolate sauce?
Ingredients for four persons
5 oz fresh maggots
2 bars of chocolate
2 oz sugar
1 oz butter
4 worm heads

Wash maggots and then place them in a frying pan, with 1 oz butter. Fry until golden brown. Then melt two bars of chocolate and add sugar and well-squashed worm heads. Pour this sauce over maggots and then put into a bowl and place in fridge until solid. A crunchy alternative for people who like a bite to things.

What did the meat say when it was about to be put on the skewer?

> *'Spear me, oh spear me!'*

Where did the baby ear of corn come from?

> *The stalk brought him.*

Why did the boy take sugar and milk to the cinema?

> *Because they were showing a serial.*

Why did the man throw the butter out of the window?

> *Because he wanted to see the butterfly.*

When should you put corn in your shoes?

> *When you have pigeon toes.*

What's chocolate outside, peanut inside and sings hymns?

> *Sunday school treet.*

What did the hamburger say to the tomato?

> *'That's enough of your sauce.'*

Eatable People

There once was a young cannibal called Ned
Who used to eat onions in bed.
His mother said 'Sonny
It's not very funny
Why don't you eat people instead?'

What did the king of the cannibals say to the famous
    missionary?
        Doctor Livingstone, I consume.

Why should you always remain calm when you meet a
    cannibal?
        Well, it's no good getting in a stew, is it?

'I don't think much of your wife.'
'Never mind – eat the vegetables instead.'

WAITER: 'Would you like the menu?'
CANNIBAL: 'No, just bring me the passenger list.'

Why did the cannibal go to the wedding reception?
        So that he could toast the guests.

What did the cannibal say when he saw the missionary
    asleep?
        'Aaaah! Breakfast in bed.'

FIRST CANNIBAL: 'Am I late for supper?'
SECOND CANNIBAL: 'Yes, everybody's eaten.'

CANNIBAL: 'How much do you charge for dinner here?'
WAITER: '£2 a head, sir.'
CANNIBAL: 'Well, I'll have a couple of legs too, please.'

FIRST CANNIBAL: 'I don't know what to make of my husband these days.'
SECOND CANNIBAL: 'How about a hotpot.'

What do cannibals play at parties?
Swallow my leader.

A cannibal came home to find his wife cutting up a boa constrictor and a small native. 'Oh no,' he said, 'not snake and pygmy pie again.'

Sickly Stitches

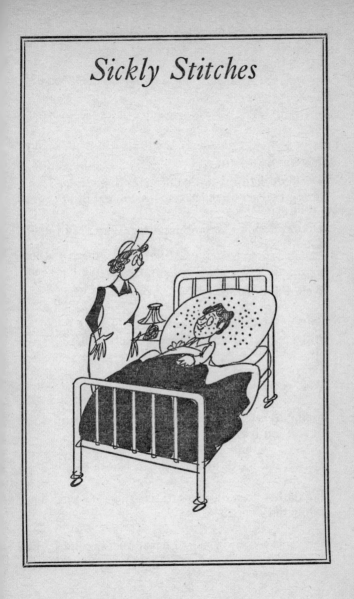

'Doc-doct-doctor, I ha-ve diff-i-cul-ty sp-eak-ing.'
'Sorry, I wasn't listening, could you repeat that?'

'Doctor, doctor, I've broken my leg. What shall I do?'
'Limp!'

'Doctor, doctor, I feel like an old sock.'
'Well, I'll be darned.'

MOLLY: 'Have your eyes ever been checked?'
POLLY: 'No, they have always been plain blue.'

'Doctor, doctor, I feel like an apple.'
'Well, come over here, I won't bite you.'

Inscription on the tombstone of a hypochondriac: 'See,
   I *told* you I was ill.'

'Doctor, doctor, this banana diet is having an odd effect
   on me.'
'For the last time, will you stop scratching and come down
   from those curtains.'

How could you say in one word that you had come across a
   doctor?
   Metaphysician.

'Doctor, doctor, I've got a terribly sore throat.'
'I see, well go over to the window and stick your tongue out.'
'That will help my throat, will it?'
'Not at all, I just don't like the neighbours.'

OPTICIAN: 'Can you read the bottom line of that chart?'
POLE: 'Read it? He's a friend of mine.'

'Nurse, what would it take to make you give me a kiss?'
'Chloroform.'

'Doctor, doctor, I get a stabbing pain in my eye every time I drink a cup of tea.'
'Have you tried taking the spoon out?'

'Doctor, doctor, I keep on seeing double.'
'Well, lie down on the couch there.'
'Yes, but which one?'

'Doctor, doctor, I feel like a horse.'
'Well, how long have you felt like this?'
'Ever since I won the 2.30 at Epsom.'

PROF. PRUNE: 'I swallowed some uranium.'
PROF. PLUM: 'What happened?'
PROF. PRUNE: 'I got atomic ache.'

'Doctor, doctor, I feel like a bar of soap.'
'That's life, boy.'

What illness do retired pilots get?
    Flu.

'Doctor, doctor, I feel like a window.
'Where's your pain?'

24

Is life worth living?
>It depends upon the liver.

Why was the doctor angry?
>He had no patients.

DOCTOR: 'Mrs Brown, you have acute paranoia.'
MRS BROWN: 'Look, I came here to be cured, not to be admired.'

'Doctor, doctor, I feel like a bell.'
'Well, take these and if they don't work give me a ring.'

Did you hear about the magician whose favourite trick was to saw a woman in half?
>She's in hospital now – in wards 9 and 10.

Did you hear about the man who fell into the lens-grinding machine and made a spectacle of himself?

What's the definition of a doctor?
>A man who suffers from good health.

What is a chiropodist's theme song?
>*There's no business like toe business.*

OPTICIAN: 'Here are your glasses. Remember you will only have to wear them when you are working.'
PATIENT: 'That might be difficult.'
OPTICIAN: 'Why, what do you do for a living?'
PATIENT: 'I'm a boxer.'

Why is a dentist always unhappy?
>*Because he looks down in the mouth.*

Nothing acts faster than Anadin.
>*So take nothing.*

'Doctor, have you got something for my kidneys?'
'Here's some bacon.'

'Doctor, will I be able to read when I get my glasses?'
'Indeed you will.'
'Well, that's fine. I never knew how to before.'

DOCTOR: 'I'm terribly sorry to tell you, Mr Smith, but you have rabies.'
MR SMITH: 'Quick, get me a pencil.'
DOCTOR: 'What for? To write a will?'
MR SMITH: 'No, to write a list of people to bite.'

'Doctor, doctor, I feel like a sheet of music.'
'Really, I must make some notes of this.'

An old lady went into the opticians and said: 'I need a new pair of glasses.'
The optician replied: 'I knew that as soon as you walked through the window.'

Hair Raisers

CUSTOMER: 'How much for a haircut?'
BARBER: 'Fifty pence.'
CUSTOMER: 'How much for a shave?'
BARBER: 'Forty pence.'
CUSTOMER: 'Right – shave my head.'

What did the bald man say when he was given a comb for
his birthday?
> *'Thank you, I'll never part with it.'*

Have you reached the age when you are losing a little on
top? Cheer up, you're probably gaining in the middle.

'Doctor, my hair is falling out. Can you give me anything
to keep it in?'
'How about a paper bag?'

What's the difference between a hairdresser and a sculptor?

> *A hairdresser curls up and dyes while a sculptor makes faces and busts.*

What is the difference between a barber in Rome and a mad circus owner?

> *One is a shaving Roman and the other a raving showman.*

My grandmother is incredible, she's ninety-two and she hasn't got a grey hair in her head. She's totally bald.

Shocking Shops

Did you hear the rumour about the watchmaker? He's just wound up his business.

What is the difference between a night watchman and a butcher?
> *One stays awake, the other weighs a steak.*

'Baker, have you any loaves left?'
'Yes, sir.'
'Well, you shouldn't have baked so many.'

'Grocer, do you have any broken biscuits?'
'Yes, madam.'
'Well, you should have been more careful then.'

CUSTOMER: 'Do you keep dripping?'
BUTCHER: 'Yes, madam.'
CUSTOMER: 'Awkward, isn't it?'

CUSTOMER: 'These mothballs you sold me are no good.'
SHOP ASSISTANT: 'Why not?'
CUSTOMER: 'I haven't hit a single moth with them.'

What is a meatball?
> *A dance in a butcher's shop.*

SHOPKEEPER: 'What would you like?'
BOY: 'A packet of bird seeds.'
SHOPKEEPER: 'What kind of bird have you?'
BOY: 'Oh, I haven't got a bird, I want to grow one with bird seeds.'

A woman who works in a sweet shop in Birmingham is 5 ft 4 ins tall. She wears size 10 shoes and her measurements are 42-26-48. What do you think she weighs?

> *Sweets!*

Growing Pains

What tree can't you climb?
> *A lavatory.*

Why did the woodman spare the tree?
> *Because he was a good feller.*

Which tree would you make a deck chair from?
> *A beech tree.*

What did the cabbages say when they knocked on the door?
> *'Lettuce in!'*

What bean isn't as good as he used to be?
> *A has been.*

What bean is made from milk?
> *A butter bean.*

What bean keeps saying 'Ooh la la'?
> *A French bean.*

MAN: 'Why do you go over the potatoes with a heavy roller?'
FARMER: 'Because I want to grow mashed potatoes.'

Which plant makes money?
Mint.

What does the garden say when it laughs?
'*Hoe, hoe, hoe.*'

What do you call an overweight pumpkin?
A plumpkin.

What do you give a hurt lemon?
Lemonade, of course.

What is long and green and always points to the North?
A magnetic cucumber.

When is it dangerous to go into a florist's shop?
When the buds are shooting.

What do you get when you plant a gun in the soil?
Lots of little shoots.

What did one strawberry say to another?
'Your freshness got us into this jam.'

What's green, hairy and wears sunglasses?
A gooseberry on holiday.

MAN: 'Why do you sow razor blades with potatoes?'
FARMER: 'Because I want to grow chips.'

What patch has no stitches?
A cabbage patch.

What vegetables do plumbers fix?
Leeks.

Ghastly Games

SEAN: 'What's blue and white and slides down the table?'
MARK: 'I don't know. What is blue and white and slides down the table?'
SEAN: 'Derby County.'

What's the best place for water skiing?
A lake with a slope.

What is the name of the team whose footballers have never met each other before the game?
Queens Park Strangers.

BOY: 'Do you know any lady football grounds?'
GIRL: 'Yes, Ann Field and Ellen Road.'

Plymouth Argyll lost all their matches so the manager brought along a demon for luck. They won against Spurs 27–0 and won against Liverpool 31–0. When the players asked why, the manager replied 'Demons are Argyll's best friend.'

When is cricket a crime?
When there is a hit and run.

IRATE GOLFER: 'Jones is a cheat – I'm not going to play with him again.'
FRIEND: 'How's that?'
GOLFER: 'Well, how could he find his lost ball on the edge of the green when it was in my pocket all the time? That proves he was a cheat.'

Why does a golfer always take a spare pair of trousers with him?

In case he gets a hole in one.

Did you hear about the tennis player who was taken to court for making a racket?

'Do you think it would be wrong of me to play golf on the sabbath, vicar?'
'The way you play it's a sin any day of the week.'

Why were the cricket team given cigarette lighters?
Because they lost all their matches.

What's green, has six legs and could kill you if it jumped
out of a tree on top of you?
A snooker table.

What ring is square?
A boxing ring.

Global Groans

What do Red Indians put on themselves after they have had a bath?
Scalpum powder.

What makes the Tower of Pisa lean?
It never eats.

If Ching Chong went to Hong Kong to play ping-pong with Ding Dong and he died, what would they put on his coffin?
A lid.

What does a Frenchman eat for breakfast?
Huit heures bix.

How does an Eskimo build his house?
'E glues it together.

What is the coldest country in the world?
Chile.

If a man is born in Turkey, grows up in Greece, goes to America and dies in London, what is he?
Dead.

What is a Laplander?
A clumsy man on a bus.

What does an Indian use to mend a hole in his trousers?
   Apache.

Checkmate – a husband or wife in Czechoslovakia.

How do you get a mid-day meal in the Alps?
   Avalanche.

Dopes and Dunces

CROSSWORD FAN: 'I've been trying to think of a word for two weeks.'
FRIEND: 'How about a fortnight?'

Do you know how you can make Paddy laugh on Boxing Day?
Tell him a joke on Christmas Eve.

One Saturday Paddy heard that the price of the *Daily Telegraph* was going up from 9p to 10p on the Monday so he went out and bought all the copies he could find.

The same man heard that the rate for first-class post was soon to go up from 9p to 10p so he went to all the Post Offices in town and bought up their entire stock of 9p stamps.

One morning I woke up and found aeroplanes in my house. Do you know why? I had left the landing light on.

'Do you like heavy or light reading, madam?'
'Oh, it doesn't matter, I've got the car outside.'

TOM: 'Did you hear about the stupid fool who goes around saying no?'
JOHN: 'No.'
TOM: 'Oh, it's you.'

There once was a lady trapped with her baby on the roof of a burning building. There was a fireman at the bottom of the building. He said to her: 'Throw down your baby and I will catch him.' The lady would not do this. Then the fireman said: 'I'm one of the best goalkeepers in the country.' So the lady threw down her baby. The fireman caught it, bounced it twice and then kicked it over a wall.

COOK: 'Elsie, why have you taken over an hour to fill that salt-cellar?'
MAID: 'I'm sorry, but the hole in the top is so small it's terribly hard to get the salt in.'

HOTEL GUEST: 'Can you give me a room and a bath?'
HOTEL CLERK: 'I can give you a room but you will have to take your own bath'

Two drunks were staggering home one night. One looked up and said: 'Is that the sun or the moon?'
His friend replied: 'I couldn't tell you, I don't live around here.'

WILF: 'I was once shipwrecked in the ocean and had to live for a week on a tin of sardines.'
ALF: 'Good job you didn't fall off.'

'Is that Dublin double two, double two?'
'No, this is Dublin 2222.'
'Oh, sorry to have bothered you.'
'That's all right, the phone was ringing anyway.'

The phone in the maternity ward rang and an excited voice said: 'I'm bringing my wife, she's going to have a baby.'
'Is this her first baby?' asked the nurse.
'No,' came the reply 'this is her husband.'

Did you hear about the bobsleigh team that refused to go down until the track was gritted?

A man went into a department store and he was just about to go up an escalator when he saw a notice saying *Dogs must be carried*. It took him an hour and a half to find a dog.

Did you hear about the man listening to a match?
He burnt his ear.

How do you keep an idiot in suspense?
I'll tell you tomorrow.

JANE: 'How are you getting on with that **guitar** you were given for your birthday?'
MIKE: 'I sent it back because there was a hole in the middle.'

A mad inventor has just perfected a new kind of tea-bag. It's waterproof.

POSTMASTER: 'Here's your 12p stamp.'
CUSTOMER (*clutching a pile of parcels*): 'Must I stick it on myself?'
POSTMASTER: 'No, silly, on the envelope.'

STUPID: 'Hello, Jim, fishing?'
DISGUSTED: 'Nope, drowning worms.'

Did you hear about the absent-minded professor who held an egg in his hand and boiled his watch?

Rotten Relations

TOM: 'When I grow up I am going to drive a tank.'
DAD: 'Well, I certainly won't stand in your way.'

MUM: 'Jimmy, did you fall over with your new trousers on?'
JIMMY: 'Yes, Mum, there wasn't time to take them off.'

MOTHER: 'What do you want to do when you're as big as your father?'
SON: 'Go on a diet.'

ELLA: 'I'm homesick.'
BELLA: 'But this is your home.'
ELLA: 'I know and I'm sick of it.'

WIFE: 'Shall I offer this tramp one of my cakes?'
HUSBAND: 'Why? What harm has he done us?'

JOHNNY: 'There's a man at the door collecting for the old people's home. Shall I give him Granny?'

DAN: 'My grandfather had a wooden leg.'
ANN: 'Well, my grandmother had a cedar chest.'

WIFE (*with camera, to husband*): 'Well, don't just stand there, get into focus.'

'What's your son going to be when he passes all his exams?'
'A pensioner.'

How do you make anti-freeze?
    Hide her nightie.

FATHER: 'Why are you crying?'
SON: 'Because my new shoes hurt.'
FATHER: 'That's because you have them on the wrong feet.'
SON: 'Well, they're the only feet I have.'

SON: 'Dad, can I have another glass of water.'
DAD: 'Another? This is your tenth.'
SON: 'I know, but my room's on fire.'

MOTHER: 'Have you given the goldfish fresh water today?'
BILLY: 'No, they haven't finished the water I gave them yesterday.'

FRED: 'Mum, can I go out and play?'
MUM: 'What! With those torn trousers?'
FRED: 'No, Mum, with the kids next door.'

What relation is a doormat to a doorstep?
   A step-father.

'Dad, there's a man at the front door with a moustache.'
'Tell him I already have one.'

What's brown, hairy, has no legs, but walks?
   Dad's socks.

Bill and Ben got a sledge for Christmas. Bill came in
   crying.
   'Now, Ben,' said their father, 'I said that you had to
   share the sledge with Bill.'
   'Yes,' said Ben, 'I had it going down and he had it
   going up.'

FATHER: 'What happened to that unbreakable, shock-
   proof, waterproof, anti-magnetic watch I gave you for
   Christmas?'
SON: 'I lost it.'

FATHER (*on Coronation Day*): 'Where is Mother, Ted?'
TED: 'Upstairs waving her hair.'
FATHER: 'Goodness, can't we afford a flag?'

What's the difference between a bad husband and a bad
   shot?
   One hits his missus and the other misses his hits.

DAD: 'Who's that at the door?'
SON: 'A man selling beehives.'
DAD: 'Well, tell him to buzz off.'

Back Chat

Is it bad to write on an empty stomach?
No, but it's better to write on paper.

'What's your name?'
'Charles, madam.'
'I always address my chauffeurs by their surname. What is it?'
'Darling, madam.'
'Drive on, Charles.'

'I'll give this pound to anybody who is quite contented.'
'I'm quite contented.'
'Then why do you want my pound?'

MIKE: 'Your new overcoat is rather loud.'
DAVE: 'It's all right, I've put on a muffler.'

A man said to a fairy: 'Do fairies have names?'
'Yes,' said the fairy, 'my name is Nuff.'
'I've never heard of that name before,' said the man.
The fairy replied, 'Surely everyone has heard of *Fairy Nuff*?'

Did you hear about Romeo and Juliet? They met in a revolving door – and they have been going round together ever since.

'I thought you were supposed to come and fix the doorbell yesterday.'
'I did, madam, I rang twice and got no answer.'

LADY SNOOKS: 'And what can I do for you, my man?'
TRAMP: 'I'd like a coat sewed on this button.'

MR JACKSON: 'Are you using your mower this afternoon?'
MR SMITH: 'Yes.'
MR JACKSON: 'Fine, then I can borrow your tennis racket. You won't be needing it.'

'You remind me of a man.'
  'What man?'
'The man with the power.'
  'What power?'
'The power of "oo-do".'
  'Who do?'
'You do.'
  'I do what?'
'Remind me of a man.'
  'What man?'
'The man with the power . . .'

Did you hear about the two paint tankers – one carrying red paint and the other blue paint – which collided in the sea? The crew are said to be 'marooned'.

FIRST MAN: 'There's a man outside with a nasty look on his face.'
SECOND MAN: 'Tell him you've already got one.'

JACK: 'Do you believe in free speech?'
MARY: 'Certainly I do.'
JACK: 'Good, may I use your telephone?'

MAN: 'Every time I'm down in the dumps I buy a new suit.'
WOMAN: 'So that's where you get those awful things from.'

'Je t'adore,' he whispered passionately in her ear.
'Shut it yourself,' she shouted back at him.

ARABELLA: 'You would be a fine dancer except for two things.'
ARCHIBALD: 'What are they?'
ARABELLA: 'Your feet!'

Name the world's most shocking city.
        Electricity.

In the Drink

There was a man in a pub who had only one arm and he was trailing his empty sleeve in another man's drink. This man said: 'Your sleeve is trailing in my drink!' The other man said: 'Well, there isn't any 'arm in it.'

Did you hear about the millionaire who hated washing? He was filthy rich.

What part of a ship is strict?
    The stern part.

What did the mummy sardine say to her child when they saw a submarine?
    'Don't worry, it's only a tin of people.'

Why did the fish blush?
    Because the sea weed.

Why does the ocean roar?
    So would you if you had crabs on your bottom.

Why is Wales covered in water?
    Because there are so many leeks in it.

Why did the sailor grab a bar of soap when his ship sank?
    To wash himself ashore.

Why should fish be better educated than mice?
> *Because they live in schools.*

What is the wettest animal in the world?
> *Reindeer.*

SOPHIE: 'There's a man at the door collecting for the new swimming pool. Shall I give him a bucket of water?'

'How did you get those scars on the top of your nose?'
'From glasses.'
'Why don't you try contact lenses?'
'They don't hold enough beer.'

What do you get when you cross an ocean with happy people?
> *Waves of laughter.*

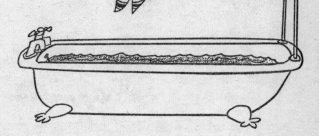

What has a mouth, and a fork, yet never eats?
> *A river.*

What is the most untidy part of a ship?
    The Officers' Mess.

A man walks into a pub and asks for a whisky. He drinks his whisky and walks out without paying. A week later he goes up to the barman and the barman says: 'You're the bloke who walked in here last week and didn't pay for your drink.'
The man replies: 'No, I'm not.'
'Well, you must have a double.'
'Thank you very much, I'll have a Scotch.'

Why are sheep like pubs?
    Because they are full of baas.

What port do ships never enter or leave?
    Davenport.

What lives under the sea and carries lots of people?
    An octobus.

What does the sea say to the sand?
    Nothing, it just waves.

When is a bucket ill?
>*When it is a little pail.*

When is the Navy like a cruet?
>*When the salts are mustered to pepper the enemy.*

'Excuse me, I'm a stranger here. Where's the nearest
  boozer?'
'You're looking at him.'

Three old ladies were walking along the road under an
  umbrella with holes in it. Why didn't they get wet?
>*Because it wasn't raining.*

A man goes into a pub with a friend and says: 'I'll have a
  beer for Donkey and me.'
The barman gives them their beers and says to the friend:
  'Why does he call you Donkey?'
He replies: 'Eeyore, eeyore, eeyore ee always calls me
  that.'

Teaching Terrors

What is the difference between teachers and Polo mints?
    People like Polos.

TEACHER: 'Have you read *Freckles*?'
BOY: 'No, I have the brown kind.'

What is the most popular phrase at school?
    '*I don't know.*'

TEACHER: Give me a sentence with the word "judicious"
    in it.'
BOY: 'Please, miss – "hands that judicious can be as soft
    as your face".'

PUPIL: 'Did you know that the most intelligent person in
    the world was going deaf?'
TEACHER: 'Really, who is it?'
PUPIL: 'Pardon?'

TEACHER: 'You missed school yesterday, didn't you?'
PUPIL: 'Not a bit, sir.'

Sam had just completed his first day at school. 'What did
you learn today?' asked his mother.
'Not enough,' said Sam. 'I have to go back tomorrow.'

Poor old teacher. We missed you so
When into hospital you did go.
For you to remain would be a sin,
We're sorry about the banana skin.

TEACHER: 'Order, children, order.'
PUPIL: 'I'll have an ice-cream and jelly please.'

PETER: 'Why don't you take the bus home?'
SAM: 'No thanks, my mum would only make me bring it
    back.'

TEACHER: 'Which month has 28 days?'
PUPIL: 'They all have.'

JOAN: 'What do you know about the Dead Sea, Jane?'
JANE: 'I didn't even know it was ill.'

BIG BROTHER: 'Well, Joe, how do you like school?'
JOE: 'Closed.'

TEACHER (*to tardy student*): 'Why are you late?'
BARRY: 'Well, a sign down the street said . . .'
TEACHER: 'Now what can a sign possibly have to do with
    it?'
BARRY: 'The sign said "School ahead go slow".'

64

TEACHER: 'New boy, tell me your name.'
BOY: 'John Mickey Smith.'
TEACHER: 'I'll call you John Smith.'
BOY: 'My dad won't like that.'
TEACHER: 'Why not?'
BOY: 'He doesn't like people taking the Mickey out of my name.'

TOM: 'Dad, I've got good news.'
DAD: 'Have you passed your exams?'
TOM: 'No, not exactly, but I was top of those who failed.'

TEACHER: 'Little girl, are your parents in?'
LITTLE GIRL: 'They was in but now they is out.'
TEACHER: 'Where's your grammar?'
LITTLE GIRL: 'In the front room watching TV.'

TEACHER: 'Which one of you can use "fascinate" in a proper sentence?'
JIMMY: 'Please, teacher, I can.'
TEACHER: 'All right, Jimmy, go ahead.'
JIMMY: 'My raincoat has ten buttons on it but I can only fasten eight.'

What exams does Santa Claus take?
    Ho! Ho! Ho! levels

Why did the boy take an axe to school?
    It was breaking-up day.

Historical Horrors

Why did the Romans build straight roads?
> *So the Britons couldn't hide round the corners.*

What sort of lighting did Noah put in his Ark?
> *Flood lighting.*

RON: 'Napoleon conquered France, conquered Russia and conquered Italy.'
BOB: 'Why did he stop?'
RON: 'Because he ran out of conkers.'

Why didn't they play cards on Noah's Ark?
> *Because Noah sat on the deck.*

What is the difference between Noah's Ark and Joan of Arc?
> *One was made of wood and the other was Maid of Orleans.*

What was Noah's job?
> *Preserving pears.*

Where did Noah keep his bees?
> *In the archives.*

What bus sailed the ocean?
> *Columbus.*

Who was the most popular person in the Bible?
Samson. He brought the house down.

Who is known as the chiropodist king?
William the Corncurer.

JILL: 'Why did Henry VIII have so many wives?'
KATE: 'I don't know.'
JILL: 'Because he liked to chop and change.'

Loopy Letters and Dotty Digits

What do you get if you dial 765043918256430991866600?
    A blister on your finger.

What's in the middle of Paris?
    R.

What two letters spell jealousy?
    NV.

How can you tell Ellen she is pretty in just eight letters?
    URABUTLN.

What word minus a letter makes you sick?
    Music.

Describe in one word 962 little cakes dancing.
    Abundance.

How do you spell 'blind pig' with two letters?
    PG (pig without an eye).

What is the end of everything?
    The letter G.

Is there a word in the English language that contains all the
  vowels?
    Unquestionably!

Which word is always spelt wrongly?
    Wrongly.

What letter is never found in the alphabet?
    The one that is lost in the post.

How do you make a witch itch?
    Take off the W.

How many weeks belong to a year?
    Forty-six, the other six are lent.

How can you make a tea table into a meal?
    Take away T and it becomes eatable.

What's the difference between a wizard and the letters
  KEMAS?
    One makes spells and the other spells makes.

Things you never saw
A shoe box
A salad bowl
A square dance

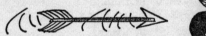

A question of logic
Darts fly like arrows
Fruit flies like bananas

What has four i's and a mouth?
    The Mississippi.

Why is the letter E lazy?
Because it is always in bed.

When can a donkey be spelled in one letter?
When it's U.

What's the French for an idiot?
Lagoon.

What letter travels the greatest distance?
D, because it goes to the end of the world.

If two is company, three is a crowd, what is four and five?
Nine.

What ends with E and begins with P and has a thousand letters?
Post Office.

Why is an island like T?
They are both in the middle of water.

Q.: How many seconds in a minute?
A.: 60.
Q.: How many seconds in a year?
A.: 12. 2 January, 2 February, 2 March and so on.

How do you pronounce VOLIX?
Volume nine.

What is bigger when it is upside down?
The number 6.

What letters are most like a Roman Emperor?
The C's are.

When did only three vowels exist?
Before U and I were born.

Why is the letter V like an angry bull?
Because it comes after U.

Abandon   What a big fat cigar has
Adore   Something you walk through
Ball   Make a lot of noise
Barbecue   Line up for a hair cut
Buoyant   Brother of a sister ant

Emulate   Dead emu
Hatchet   What a bird tries to do when it sits on an egg
Knapsack   Sleeping bag
Knickers   Policemen
Lesson   Result of taking some clothes off
Minimum   Little mother
Shamrock   Fake diamond

Ticklish Tomes

The Working of an Electric Drill by Andy Gadget
Stand and Deliver : The Story of Dick Turpin
　by Ann Dover
Pet Owning by Ivor Dog
Bad Shooting by Miss A. Lot
Snake Breeding by Sir Pent
Sweet Making by Annie Seedball
Doubt by R. U. Sure
Bed Time by I. M. Tired
What to Use When Cooking by U. Tensils
Jelly for Tea by Eileen Joyit
Who Saw Him Leave by Wendy Go
Say Your Prayers by Neil Down
Something for the Toast by Marjorie Nisgood
The Winner by Vic Tree
The Two Of Us by Ewan Me
Sorry Not Possible by Fred I. Kant
Help for a Jail Breaker by Freda Prisner
Sahara Journey by I. Rhoda Camel
The Painter by R. T. Stick
Loud Rumblings by M. T. Tumm
Making Merry by Hans Neesanboompsadaisy
Old Furniture by Ann Teak
Au Revoir by C. U. Later
Splitting the Atom by Molly Cule
Central Heating by Ray D. Ator
Order in School by Emma Prefect

I must not write on walls
I must not write on walls
I must not write on walls
I must not write on walls
I must not write on walls
I must not write on walls
I must not write on walls
I must not write on

Ghosts by R. U. Scared
How to Improve Your Memory by I. Forgot
Golf by A. Par
A Hole in One by A. Goodshot
All About Dogs by K. Nine
Astronomy by I. C. Stars
Dinosaurs by Terry Dacktill
Angel Choirs by Hal E. Looyah
Army Humour by Major Laff
Short Measurements by Milly Metre
Bell Ringing by Paula Rope
The World of Vegetables by R. T. Choke
Compost by D. K. Ing
Winds by Gail Force II
One Hundred Yards to the Bus Stop by Willy Makitt,
    illustrated by Betty Wont
The Fat Stomach by Henrietta Lott
Long Necked Animals by G. Raff

The Army Way by Reggie Mental
School Dinners by R. E. Volting
The Great Mystery by Ivor Clue
How to Feed Monkeys by P. Nuts
Falling off a Ladder by Mister Step
Early One Morning by R. U. Upjohn
Ten Years in a Monkey House by Bab Boone
Bricks and Mortar by Bill Ding
All About Explosives by Dinah Mite
Food on the Plate by E. Tittup
The Flower Garden by Polly Anthus
Tea for Two by Roland Butta
The Unhappy Restaurant by Sad Café
Talk by Hot Gossip
I'm Down by Nick Lowe
How To Be Bright by The Electric Light Orchestra
Greenfingers by Kate Bush
Sandy by The Beach Boys

Potty Pomes and Loathsome Limericks

Nobody loves me, everybody hates me
I'm going in the garden to eat worms.
Long slim slimy ones,
Short fat fuzzy ones,
Gooey – ooey – ooey ones.
The long slim slimy ones slip down easily,
The short fat fuzzy ones stick to your teeth,
And make you go urr urr yum yum.

> A Professor named Alistair Quett
> Said, 'Three things I always forget.
> There's all my friends' names,
> And the times of my trains
> And the third one I can't recall yet.'

There was a young lady called Maud
Who was the most terrible fraud.
To eat when at table,
She never was able
But when in the larder, oh, gawd!

> There once was a man from Darjeeling
> Who boarded a bus bound for Ealing.
> It said on the door
> Please don't spit on the floor
> So he stood up and spat on the ceiling.

There was a young man from Crewe
Who wanted to build a canoe.
He got to the river
And found with a shiver
He hadn't used waterproof glue.

During dinner at the Ritz
Father kept on having fits.
And, which made my sorrow greater,
I was left to tip the waiter.

There was a small goldfish named Pinkie
Who went for a swim in the sinkie.
When out came the plug
He whispered 'glug, glug
I'll be all at sea in a winkie.'

Mary had a little lamb
You've heard this tale before
But did you know
She passed her plate
And had a little more?

There was a young lady of Diss
Who thought skating was absolute bliss
Till love turned to hate
When a slip of her skate
Made her finish up something like this.

There was an old woman from
    China
Who went to sea on a liner.
She fell off the deck
And twisted her neck
And now can see right behind
    her.

There once was a lady named Rose
Who had an extremely long nose.
When she walked around
It would drag on the ground
And get tangled up with her toes.

> 'Twas in a restaurant they met,
> Romeo and Juliet.
> He had no cash to pay the debt
> So Romeo'd what Juliet

There was a young man from Bengal
Who wanted to go to a fancy dress ball.
He thought he would risk it
And go as a biscuit
But a dog ate him up in the hall.

> The rain makes all things beautiful,
> The flowers and grasses too.
> If rain makes things beautiful
> Why don't it rain on you?

There was an old man of Vancouver
Whose wife got sucked into the hoover.
He said 'There's some doubt
If she's more in than out
But whichever it is I can't move her.'

> *Epitaph*
> Here lies a chump who got no gain
> From jumping on a moving train.
> Banana skins on platform seven
> Ensured his terminus was Heaven.

Ooey gooey was a worm, a wondrous worm was he.
He stepped upon a railway line, a train he did not see.
Ooey, gooey.

There once was a lady from Ealing
Who just couldn't stop herself squealing.
She squealed to the cat
Who tripped over the mat
And the scar on its head is now healing.

Old Tom is gone (too soon alas!)
He tried to trace escaping gas.
With lighted match he braved the fates
Which blew him to the Pearly Gates.

Little Miss Muffet
Sat on her tuffet
Eating her Irish stew.
Along came a spider
And sat down beside her
So she ate him up too.

Mr Window Cleaner, you'll soon be well
After all, it wasn't far you fell.
You certainly received a nasty crack
Don't worry though you'll get your ladder
  back.

We three kings of Orient are,
One in a taxi, one in a car,
One on a scooter, peeping his hooter,
Following yonder star.

Here rests the body of our M.P.
Who promised lots for you and me.
His words his deeds did not fulfil
And though he's dead he's LYING STILL.

There once was a young man called Frank
Who invented a new kind of tank.
He said it would float
Just like a boat
But the first time he tried it, it sank.

I had written to Aunt Maud,
Who was on a trip abroad,
When I heard she'd died of cramp
Just too late to save the stamp.

A jovial fellow named Packer
Pulled out a joke from his cracker.
It said: 'If you're stuck
For a turkey, try duck –
You could say it's a real Christmas Quacker.'

There was once a boy from Looe
Who dreamt he had eaten his shoe.
He woke up in the night
With a terrible fright
And found it was perfectly true!

A fellow named Arthur McNares
Kept a number of grizzly bears.
They ate so much honey
He ran out of money
So then they ate Arthur – who cares?

I sat next to the duchess at tea,
It was just as I feared it would be.
Her rumblings abdominal
Were simply phenomenal
And everyone thought it was me!

Epitaph
Here lies a man who met his fate
Because he put on too much weight.
To over-eating he was prone
But now he's gained his final STONE.

Elephants You'll Never Forget

JOHN: 'What's the difference between an elephant and a matterbaby?'
PETE: 'What's a matterbaby?'
JOHN: 'Nothing, what's wrong with you?'

What is the first thing to do when an elephant breaks his toe?
> *Ring for a tow-truck.*

Why do elephants wear green felt hats?
> *So they can walk across billiard tables without being seen.*

Why does an elephant have wrinkled feet?
> *To give the ants half a chance.*

IRV: 'How do you tell an elephant from a banana?'
MERV: 'Try to pick it up. If you can't, it is either an elephant or a very heavy banana.'

Why does an elephant wear plimsolls?
> *To sneak up on mice.*

Why do elephants wear sandals?
> *To stop themselves sinking in the sand.*

Why do ostriches bury their heads?
>*To look for elephants who have not been wearing sandals.*

JOHN: 'What's the difference between a flea, an elephant and a lollipop?'
PETE: 'I don't know; what is the difference between a flea, an elephant and a lollipop?'
JOHN: 'Elephants can have fleas, but fleas can't have elephants.'
PETE: 'But what about the lollipop?'
JOHN: 'That's a sucker for someone like you.'

What do you get when you cross an elephant with a goldfish?
>*Swimming trunks.*

Slithery Sniggers

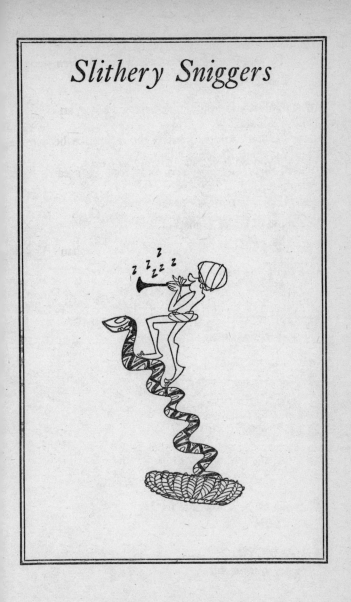

What do you do if you catch a slippery eel?
Nothing, because you can't catch a slippery eel – it's too slippery.

What type of snake is good at sums?
An adder.

Why can't you fool a snake?
Because he hasn't a leg to pull.

What's white outside, green inside and hops?
A frog sandwich.

What happens when a frog's van breaks down?
It gets toad away.

What is green and goes dit dit dot dot?
A morse toad.

What did the python say to its victim?
'I've got a crush on you.'

What is a snake's favourite food?
Hiss fingers.

How do frogs die?
They Kermit suicide.

What happened to the snake with a cold?
She adder viper nose.

What is a frog's favourite flower?
A croakus.

Where do frogs fly their flags?
On the tad pole.

What's green and turns red at the flick of a switch?
A frog in a liquidizer.

Mad Menageries

Why does a lion have a fur coat?
Because he would look ridiculous in a plastic mac.

Why is your dog so angry?
Because he's got distemper.

Why did the horse gallop over the hill?
Because he couldn't gallop under it.

Why are clouds like people on horseback?
They both hold rains.

Where does Tarzan get his clothes from?
A jungle sale.

What is the highest form of animal life?
A giraffe.

What do hedgehogs eat for breakfast?
Prickled onions.

What did the horse say when he got to the end of his nose-bag?
'That's the last straw.'

What otter can travel very fast?
An otter-mobile.

What unlocks a Turkish house?
A turkey.

How does a motorist get a sheep to look round?
He makes a ewe turn.

'I'm very sorry, lady, but I have just run over your cat.
I'd like to replace it.'
'How are you at catching mice?'

What do you get if you cross a gun dog with a telephone?
A golden receiver.

What did the parrot do after it swallowed an alarm clock?
Became a politician.

What do you get if you cross an owl with a skunk?
A bird that smells but doesn't give a hoot.

PADDY: 'I've just bought a pig.'
SAM: 'Where are you going to keep it?'
PADDY: 'Under my bed.'
SAM: 'What about the smell?'
PADDY: 'Oh, it won't mind that.'

Did you hear about the worm who had Egyptian flu?
Yes, he caught it from his mummy.

What is the biggest cow in Russia?
Moscow.

What dog looks like a flower?
A collieflower.

Why do giraffes have long necks?
To connect their heads to their bodies.

What did the grizzly take on holiday?
All the bear essentials.

LUCY: 'Is it correct to say that you water your horse?'
MOTHER: 'Yes, dear.'
LUCY: 'Then I'm going out to milk the cat.'

What animal eats the least?
The moth – it just eats holes.

Where do you find the most fish?
Between the head and the tail.

Why are goldfish red?
The water makes them rusty.

Did you hear about the jelly fish?
>*It set.*

What do you get when you cross a cocoa bean with an elk?
>*Chocolate moose.*

How can you recognize a rabbit stew?
>*It has hares in it.*

PASSER-BY: 'Is this river good for fish?'
FISHERMAN: 'It must be. I can't get any of them to leave it.'

What do you get when you cross a cow, a sheep and a goat?
>*A milky bar kid.*

Why did the stag make a loaf of bread?
>*Because it kneaded the doe.*

What would happen if pigs could fly?
>*Bacon would go up.*

Why did the boy call his dog 'Sandwich'?
Because it was half-bred.

A lady hired two workmen to fit her living-room carpet. When they had finished, one noticed a square bulge under the carpet, right in the middle of the floor. 'Oh no,' he said, 'I must have left my cigarettes on the floor. Well, I'm not going to take all that lot up again.' So he got a hammer and squashed the lump flat so that it looked as if nothing was under the carpet.

At that moment the lady came in with cups of tea and said, 'Well, you've done a good job and I've found your cigarettes in the kitchen. By the way, have you seen my escaped hamster anywhere?'

What is the hardest part of milking a mouse?
Getting a bucket under it.

If cheese comes after dinner, what comes after cheese?
A mouse.

A bird in the hand makes it difficult to wipe your nose.

What's green and swings through the trees in Africa?
>*A septic monkey.*

When is a fish pond like a bird cage?
>*When there's a perch in it.*

What's yellow and smells of bananas?
>*Monkey puke.*

SCIENTIST: 'I've just crossed a hyena with a man-eating tiger.'
ASSISTANT: 'What did you get?'
SCIENTIST: 'I'm not sure; but when he laughs you'd better join in.'

TOM: 'What has four legs and flies?'
TIM: 'I don't know, what has got four legs and flies?'
TOM: 'A dead horse.'

What did the ant say to the bee?
>   *'Your honey or your life.'*

PASSENGER IN PLANE: 'Look at those people down there, they look just like ants.'
PILOT: 'They are ants ... We haven't left the ground yet.'

What wig can hear?
>   *An earwig.*

Where do spiders play football?
>   *Webley.*

What is the biggest moth of all?
>   *A mam-moth.*

JIMMY: 'Dad, what has a purple spotted body, ten hairy legs and big eyes on stalks?'
DAD: 'I don't know, why?'
JIMMY: 'One's crawling up your trouser leg.'

Why did the ant elope?
>   *Nobody gnu.*

Why did the ants run along the biscuit box?
>   *Because the instructions said 'Tear along the dotted line'.*

Why do bees buzz?
>   *Because they can't whistle.*

'I've just been stung by one of your bees.'
'Well, show me which one it was and I'll see that it's punished.'

What is the difference between a weasel and a stoat?
*A weasel is weasily recognized and a stoat is stoataly
different.*

What should you do if you find a gorilla asleep in your
bed?
Sleep somewhere else.

What is it called when you kill a pig?
Hamicide.

MAN: 'Can I have a parrot for my son please?'
PET-SHOP OWNER: 'Sorry, sir, we don't swop.'

What do bees say in the summer?
       '*Swarm.*'

JILL: 'A man was walking through a jungle and a pintcost
    came out and bit him.'
BILL: 'What's a pintcost?'
JILL: 'About 50p.'

What is the best year for kangaroos?
       Leap year.

Why is there an eagle on a lectern in church?
> *Because it is a bird of prey.*

What did the porcupine say to the cactus?
> *'Is that you, Mama?'*

What do geese watch on TV?
> *Duckumentaries.*

TIM: 'That old shack's a wreck. I wonder what keeps it from falling down?'
JIM: 'The woodworms must be holding hands!'

Why did Little Bo-Peep lose her sheep?
> *She had a crook with her.*

What did the mouse say when it broke some of its front teeth?
> *'Hard cheese.'*

HIM: 'There I was, unarmed. Wild horses in front of me, lions and tigers by my side. A pack of wolves behind me.'
ME: 'So what did you do?'
HIM: 'I got off the roundabout.'

One mouse fell off the wall, what did the other mouse do?
> *He used mouse-to-mouse resuscitation.*

Why is a horse like a cricket match?
> *Because it gets stopped by the rein.*

Where do parrots with three A-levels go?
> *A polly technic.*

Which horses have the shortest legs?
The smallest ones.

What do you call a female goat?
A buttress.

How can you close an envelope under
water?
With a seal, of course.

What did they call the baby bear that was born bald?
Fred bear.

Why couldn't the butterfly go to the dance?
Because it was a mothball.

Shaggy Dogs

Chinese boy

An old Chinese man is walking down the road when he comes across a small Chinese boy who is cutting his nails.

OLD MAN: 'Little boy, stop cutting your nails!'

The small boy looks up at him and then carries on cutting his nails.

OLD MAN: 'Little boy, I say, you stop cutting your nails!'

Again, the boy looks up at him and then continues cutting his nails.

OLD MAN: 'Little boy, why when I have told you to stop cutting your nails do you carry on?'

SMALL BOY: 'Because my neighbours beat their child.'

OLD MAN: 'But what has that got to do with you cutting your nails?'

SMALL BOY: 'What has cutting my nails got to do with you?'

Orange peel

STORYTELLER: 'A hiker was walking down a road when he sprained his ankle. Luckily a monk found him and took him to his monastery, where he said: "You can stay the night but don't look out of the window at twelve o'clock." The hiker stayed at the monastery but he looked out of the window at twelve o' clock and saw a piece of orange peel. In the morning he asked the monk what the orange peel was doing. The monk said:

"You have to be a monk to find out." So the hiker enrolled to be a monk and the other monk took him down a long dark passage, then opened a door and the monk who had been a hiker saw ...

LISTENER: 'Saw what?'

STORYTELLER: 'You have to be a monk to find out.'

Polar bears

There was once a family of polar bears – father bear, mother bear and baby bear. One day baby bear said to his mother: 'Mum, am I a true polar bear?'

His mother said to him: 'Yes, son, you are.'

Baby bear then said: 'Am I 100 per cent polar bear?'

His mother then said to him: 'Well, why don't you ask your father?'

So the baby bear went to see his father. Father bear was on a huge ice-berg looking out to sea. Baby bear struggled up the ice-berg and said to his father: 'Dad, dad, am I a true polar bear?'

Then father bear said to his son: 'Yes, son, you are.'
Baby bear then said 'One hundred per cent polar bear?'
Father bear answered: 'Yes, son.'
Baby bear then said: 'Then why am I so flippin' cold?'

Toasties
There was once a rabbit walking down the road. Suddenly he felt rather hungry. Luckily he saw, across the road, a public house. He walked in and went straight up to the bar. 'Do you serve anything to eat?' he asked the barman, very politely.

'Well, as it happens,' said the barman, 'today we are serving toasties, ham toasties, cheese toasties and tomato toasties . . .'

'Lovely,' said the rabbit, 'I'll have a pint of bitter and a ham toastie.' So he took his drink and his toastie to the corner table. When he had finished, he still felt hungry and so went back to the bar. 'I'll have another pint and a cheese toastie,' and he took his drink and his toastie back to the table. He still felt hungry when he had finished these and so returned to the bar. 'I'll have another pint and a tomato toastie, please.' And he returned to his corner seat. He finished these. By now, as he was only a rabbit with a very weak head, he was well and truly drunk. The barman went to throw him out but the rabbit had no sooner stood up than he fell down again, dead. The barman considered rabbit stew, but, no, the rabbit had been a good customer. So the barman buried him in the back garden.

The next night everyone was in the bar drinking when, through the wall, came the ghost of the rabbit. All the customers ran out screaming. But the barman, stuck behind the bar, could not get out and so was squashed up against the wall, as far away from the ghost as possible.

'Was there anything wrong with the drink?' he asked, nervously.

'No,' replied the ghost.

'What did you die of then?' he asked, and the rabbit replied: 'Mixin' matoasties!'

Heaven to Hell

There once were two boys – Sanfran and James. Sanfran was bad and James was good, but they were the best of friends. When they died Sanfran went to Hell and James to Heaven. There were phones in Heaven and Hell so James phoned Sanfran. Sanfran asked what it was like in Heaven and James said it was terrible. He had to take the stars in, polish them and put them back out again and he also had to get up very early. James asked Sanfran what it was like in Hell. Sanfran said it was great – there were women, drink and discos. Sanfran asked if James could come down to Hell for a day. James said he would ask God. God said yes but he would have to take his harp. So he went to Hell and met Sanfran and they went to a disco. They had a really good time and soon the day was over. When James got back to Heaven, God asked him where his harp was.

James replied: 'I left my harp in Sanfran's disco.'

Teddy bear

A teddy bear used to work on a building site until the following happened to him.

One day he was digging away with his pickaxe when the bell went for lunch. He came back to find his pick had gone so he went up to the foreman and said: 'My pick has been taken.' And the foreman replied: 'Don't you know, today's the day the teddy bears have their pick nicked.'

Aladdin's lamp

There once was a man, who found Aladdin's lamp. He rubbed the lamp and out came a genie.

'You have three wishes.'

'My first wish is that I could have a glass and a bottle of Guinness and, when you pour it out, the bottle fills up again.'

The genie said 'Right,' and gave it to him.

He tried it and it worked and he said, 'I will have two more bottles, then.'

Knock, Knock

Knock, knock.
Who's there?
Dishwasher.
Dishwasher who?
Dishwasher the way I
   spoke before I had
   my false teeth.

Knock, knock.
Who's there?
Henrietta and Juliet.
Henrietta and Juliet
   who?
Henrietta dinner and
   feels ill.
Juliet the same but is
   O.K.

Knock, knock.
Who's there?
Mr.
Mr who?
Mr last bus home.

Knock, knock.
Who's there?
Ivor.
Ivor who?
Ivor sore hand from
   knocking on your
   door.

Knock, knock.
Who's there?
Ivan.
Ivan who?
Ivan idea you don't
   want to let me in.

Knock, knock.
Who's there?
Howard.
Howard who?
Howard I know.

Knock, knock.
Who's there?
Mayonnaise.
Mayonnaise who?
Mayonnaise have seen
   the glory of the
   coming of the Lord.

Knock, knock.
Who's there?
Ivor.
Ivor who?
Ivor a good mind not to
   tell you.

Knock, knock.
Who's there?
Elsie.
Elsie who?
Elsie you later.

Knock, knock.
Who's there?
Alex.
Alex who?
Alex plain later.

Knock, knock.
Who's there?
Anne.
Anne who?
Anne apple just fell on
   my head.

Knock, knock.
Who's there?
Frances.
Frances who?
Frances capital is Paris.

Knock, knock.
Who's there?
Toodle.
Toodle who?
Bye.

Knock, knock.
Who's there?
Euripedes.
Euripedes who?
Euripedes and you'll
   pay for a new pair.

Knock, knock.
Who's there?
Brother.
Brother who?
Brotherhood of Man.

Knock, knock.
Who's there?
Arena.
Arena who?
Arenavation is needed
   on this here doorbell.

Knock, knock.
Who's there?
Olive.
Olive who?
I love you too, honey.

Knock, knock.
Who's there?
Martin.
Martin who?
Martin of beans won't
  open!

Knock, knock.
Who's there?
Shelby.
Shelby who?
Shelby coming round
  the mountain.

Knock, knock.
Who's there?
Mahatma.
Mahatma who?
Mahatma coat please.

KNOCK
KNOCK

Knock, knock.
Who's there?
Ali.
Ali who?
Alleluyah, at last you've
  answered the door.

Knock, knock.
Who's there?
Horace.
Horace who?
Horace scopes can be
  fun.

Knock, knock.
Who's there?
Musket.
Musket who?
Musket in.

Knock, knock.
Who's there?
Viola.
Viola who?
Viola sudden you don't
  know me?

Knock, knock.
Who's there?
Des.
Des who?
Des no door bell, that's
  why I'm knocking.

Knock, knock.
Who's there?
Theodore.
Theodore who?
Theodore is shut. Come
  down and let me in.

Knock, knock.
Who's there?
Monsieur.
Monsieur who?
Monsieur ask so many
  questions?

Knock, knock.
Who's there?
Ammonia.
Ammonia who?
Ammonia little boy who
  can't reach the
  doorbell.

Knock, knock.
Who's there?
Owen.
Owen who?
Owen are you going to
    let me out.

Knock, knock.
Who's there?
Wood.
Wood who?
Wood you believe
I've forgotten?

Knock, knock.
Who's there?
Amos.
Amos who?
Amosquito.

Knock, knock.
Who's there?
Wendy.
Wendy who?
Wendy next stupid
    mosquito comes
    I'll kill it.

Knock, knock.
Who's there?
Solly.
Solly who?
Solly you been troubled.
    Me makee mistake.

Knock, knock.
Who's there?
Willoughby.
Willoughby who?
Willoughby be quick
    and open the door?

IF AT FIRST
YOU DON'T
SUCCEED
TRY, TRY, AGAIN

Knock, knock.
Who's there?
Eggs.
Eggs who?
Eggstremely nice to
    meet you.

Knock, knock.
Who's there?
Four eggs.
Four eggs who?
Four eggsample.

Knock, knock.
Who's there?
Buster.
Buster who?
Buster school, please.

Knock, knock.
Who's there?
Police.
Police who?
Police open up, thank
you.

Knock, knock.
Who's there?
Fozzie.
Fozzie who?
Fozzie hundredth time
my name is Paul!

Knock, knock.
Who's there?
Don.
Don who?
Don just mess about,
open the door.

Knock, knock.
Who's there?
Jester.
Jester who?
Jester minute and I'll
find out.

Knock, knock.
Who's there?
Santa.
Santa who?
Santa forward in our
    team was ill today.

Knock, knock.
Who's there?
Cook.
Cook who?
Oh, I didn't know it was
    one o'clock already.

Knock, knock.
Who's there?
Noah.
Noah who?
Noah good place to eat?

Knock, knock.
Who's there?
Sob, sob, boo.
Sob, sob, boo, who?
There's no need to cry,
    it's only a joke.

Knock, knock.
Who's there?
Phyllis.
Phyllis who?
Phyllis a glass of water,
    I'm thirsty.

Knock, knock.
Who's there?
Disease.
Disease who?
Disease trousers fit you?

Knock, knock.
Who's there?
Jackson.
Jackson who?
Jackson the telephone!

Knock, knock.
Who's there?
Andrew.
Andrew who?
Andrew a lovely picture
    today.

Knock, knock.
Who's there?
Butcher.
Butcher who?
Butcher right arm in . . .

Knock, knock.
Who's there?
Noah.
Noah who?
Noah don't know who
    you are either.

Knock, knock.
Who's there?
Wendy.
Wendy who?
Wendy joke is over you
   had better laugh.

Knock, knock.
Who's there?
Lemmy.
Lemmy who?
Lemmy in and I'll tell
   you.

Knock, knock.
Who's there?
Colin.
Colin who?
Colin the doctor, I'm
   ill.

Knock, knock.
Who's there?
Sonya.
Sonya who?
Sonya foot, I can smell
   it from here.

Knock, knock.
Who's there?
Violet.
Violet who?
Violet you know, you'll
   tell someone else.

Knock, knock.
Who's there?
Havelock.
Havelock who?
Havelock put on your
   door.

Knock, knock.
Who's there?
Major.
Major who?
Major answer, didn't I?

Knock, knock.
Who's there?
Mandy.
Mandy who?
Mandy lifeboats, we're
   sinking.

Knock, knock ting-a-ling.
Who's there?
UCI.
UCI who?'
UCI had to ring
   because you didn't
   answer when I
   knocked.

Knock, knock.
Who's there?
Signor.
Signor who?
Signor light on.

Knock, knock.
Who's there?
Wicked.
Wicked who?
Wicked make beautiful
   music together.

Knock, knock.
Who's there?
Huron.
Huron who?
Huron time for once.

Star Screamers

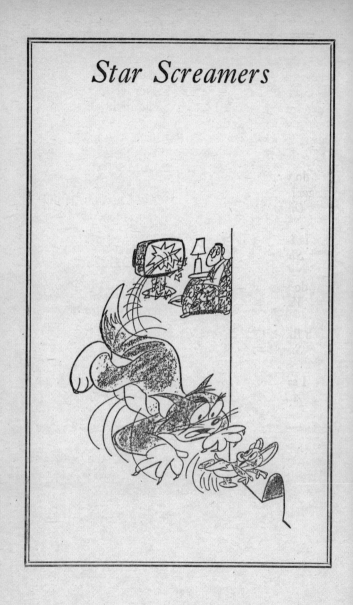

What do you get if you cross a wild animal with a famous singer?
  Dingo Starr.

What is Hissing Sid's favourite football team?
  Slitherpool.

What do you call a bald Cheshire cat?
  Yul grinner.

Which Radio One disc-jockey may go fishing?
  Simon Bates.

I say, I say, I say. How many ears has Captain Kirk got?
  A left ear, a right ear, and a final frontier!

A man went into a bank and said: 'Please may I arrange a loan?'
'I'm afraid the loan arranger isn't in, sir,' the bank clerk replied.
'Then who should I see?' asked the man.
'Tonto.'

Three men went for an audition for Star Trek.
The first man who went in had pointed ears and said he
would like to play the role of Spock.
The second was a Chinaman and he asked to play Sulu.
The third man went in dressed as a tree.
'What part do you want to play?' asked the producer.
'The Captain's log,' came the reply.

What is big and green and sits in the corner all day?
The Incredible Sulk.

What howls hysterically in Coronation Street?
Hyena Sharples.

What is a cow's favourite TV programme?
Dr Moo.

Which Radio One disc-jockey is interested in books?
Mike Read.

What do you call a couple of comedians who can cure
indigestion?
The Two Rennies.

What's green, round and smells?
Kermit's bottom.

Cryptic Chuckles

What's Dracula's favourite society?
The Consumers' Association.

What do devils drink?
Demonade.

Why do demons and ghouls get along so well?
Because demons are a ghoul's best friend.

What do you call a kind-hearted, neat, handsome monster?
A failure.

What do you call a ghost doctor?
A surgical spirit.

LITTLE BOY: 'Mummy, what's a werewolf?'
MOTHER: 'Be quiet and comb your face.'

A ghoul stood on the bridge one night,
Its lips were all a-quiver.
It gave a cough,
Its leg fell off
And floated down the river.

1937 Hearse for sale.
Body still in good condition.

What is a monster's favourite soup?
Scream of tomato.

Why are vampires crazy?
Because they are often bats.

Dracula films are *fangtastic*.

What jewels do ghosts wear?
Tomb stones.

What did the vampire say when he left the dentist?
'*Fangs very much.*'

What did the father ghost say to his son?
'Spook only when you are spoken to!'

Did you hear about the two blood cells?
They loved in vein!

Which monster has no luck?
The luck less monster.

What do you find in a haunted cellar?
Whines and spirits.

What is a skeleton's favourite pop group?
Boney M.

Why do we say 'Amen' and not 'Awomen'?
For the same reason as we sing hymns, not hers.

Why did Eve never fear the measles?
Because she already Adam.

Why does Santa Claus go down the chimney?
Because it soots him.

Did you hear about the man who took his car in for a service? He got it stuck in the church door.

How many wives is a man given at a marriage service?
Sixteen (four better, four worse, four richer, four poorer).

What do angry mice send each other at Christmas?
Cross-mouse cards.

One Christian to another, facing the lions in ancient Rome:
'One good thing – you don't get the crowds running
on to the pitch here.'

Where was Solomon's temple?
     Near the top of his head.

Thor, the god of thunder, went for a ride on his favourite horse.

'I'm Thor!' he cried.

'Well, you forgot your thaddle, thilly,' replied the horse.

What do you get if St Paul's Cathedral flies in the air?
An aerodome.

What do you call smoke coming out of a church?
Holy smoke.

Ask Me Another

What do punks learn at school?
Punctuation.

Why is a lawyer hardworking?
Because he works with a will.

What is the definition of a drawing pin?
A smartie poking his tongue out.

Heard the joke about the quicksand? Better not tell you -
it won't sink in.

And I expect you'd like to hear the one about the bed?
Sorry but it hasn't been made yet.

What's the quickest way to the station?
Run like mad.

What has a tail and no legs?
A kite.

Where did Humpty Dumpty put his hat?
Humpty dumped 'is 'at on the wall.

Why do you need holes in your pants?
To put your legs through.

How did Hiawatha?
>*With thoap and water.*

What books teach you to fight?
>*Scrap books.*

What colours would you paint the sun and wind?
>*The sun rose and the wind blue.*

If a buttercup is yellow, what colour is a hiccup?
>*Burple.*

What did the needle say to the thread?
>*'I've got my eye on you.'*

Why is the theatre a sad place?
>*Because the seats are always in tiers.*

What did one mind-reader say to the other one?
>*'You're all right, how am I?'*

What has a bottom at its top?
>*A leg.*

What is ten feet tall, yellow, with purple feet and sings like a nightingale?
>*Nothing.*

What happened to the boy who slept with his head under his pillow?
>*The fairies took all his teeth away.*

What did the electrician's wife say when he arrived home late?
>*Wire you insulate?*

Which burn longer – the candles on a boy's birthday cake or those on a girl's birthday cake?
No candles burn longer, they all burn shorter.

What did the pencil sharpener say to the pencil?
'Let's get to the point.'

What part of the Army could a young child join?
The Infantry.

Who wears a bowler hat and goes from branch to branch?
A bank manager.

What did Gladstone say on 1 January 1881?
'Happy New Year.'

What's the expression on an auctioneer's face?
For bidding.

What kind of fall makes you unconscious but doesn't injure you?
Falling asleep.

What do you get when you have your head chopped off?
A splitting headache.

What did one doorknob say to the other?
'Don't fly off the handle.'

What man never does a day's work?
A night watchman.

How many sides has a circle got?
Two – the inside and the outside.

What is round and bad-tempered?
A vicious circle.

What did the picture say to the wall?
'First they frame me, then they hang me.'

What is black when clean and white when dirty?
A blackboard.

What did the south wind say to the north wind?
'Let's play draughts.'

What is higher than a hill?
>*The grass that grows on it.*

What did the pen say to the paper?
>*'I dot my eyes on you.'*

Who invented the circle?
>*Sir Cumference.*

What has a ball got to do with a prince?
>*One is heir to the throne and the other is thrown into the air*

What did one loom say to the other?
>*'Let's spin a yarn.'*

What has six legs and two heads?
>*A horse and rider.*

Why do they put telephone wires on poles?
>*To keep up the conversation.*

FIRST MAN: 'There's a man on the phone selling clothes props.'
SECOND MAN: 'Tell him to hold the line.'

FIRST MAN: 'There's a man outside with a wooden leg.'
SECOND MAN: 'Tell him to hop it.'

What happened to the Irishman who went to China to work?
>*They gave him a job in the paddy fields.*

Why is a rifle like a lazy worker?
>*Because they can both get fired.*

What newspaper do cats read?
Mews of the World.

Why is a lawyer like a ballet dancer?
Because they both practise at the bar.

What did the coin say when it got stuck in the meter?
'Money's tight these days.'

What do you call a small joke?
A mini ha-ha!

When is a rope clever?
When it is taut.

Why is Sunday the strongest day?
Because all the others are weak days.

What has a neck but cannot swallow?
A bottle.

What is the best way to make a clean sweep?
Wash him.

What smells most in a chemist's shop?
Your nose.

What holds the moon up?
The moon beams.

How can you make a pound note worth more?
*If you fold it, it doubles, and when you open it again
you find it increases.*

How many sexes are there?
Three. Male, female and insects.

What is the strongest bird in the world?
A crane.

What sort of fish are afraid of dogs?
Catfish.

What do you call somebody who steals your drink?
Nick McGuinness.

What's the best system for book-keeping?
Never lend them.

What do you do when your nose goes on strike?
Picket.

What is long, horny and black?
Your toenails.

What gets wet as it dries?
A towel.

Why was the envelope on the roof?
Because it wanted ceiling.

What do you feed computers?
Silicon chips.

Why is a newspaper like an army?
It has leaders, columns and reviewers.

Why did the little ink-spots cry?
Because their mother was in the pen doing a long sentence.

What's black, white and red?
A skunk with nappy rash.

What are exams like in the Communist world?
>*You get Marx out of ten.*

What is brown on both sides and 600 feet high?
>*The Toast Office Tower!*

'What can you put in a cup but you can't take out?'
'I don't know, what can you put in a cup but you can't
take out?'
'A crack.'

What is yellow and writes underwater?
>*A ball-point banana.*

What do you get if you cross cold weather with bandages?
>*A frost-aid kit.*

What do you get if you cross a tiger and a snowman?
>*Frost bite.*

What can go round the world but still stay in one corner?
>*A postage stamp.*

What works in a circus and meows when it swings?
>*An acrocat.*

What grows in gardens, makes a sandwich and is dangerous
if you run into it?
A hambush.

What is yellow and very good at sums?
A banana with a pocket calculator.

If you tumbled downstairs what would you fall against.
Your wishes.

If a man smashed a clock, could he be accused of killing
time?
Not if the clock struck first.

When is longhand quicker than shorthand?
When it's on a clock.

Why is a watch always modest?
> *Because it is always running itself down.*

Who invented the five-day week?
> *Robinson Crusoe. He had all his work done by Friday!*

What has two hands but no fingers?
> *A clock.*

'I hear the men are striking?'
'What for?'
'Shorter hours.'
'Good luck to them. I always did think sixty minutes was too long for an hour.'

What are musicians supposed to wear?
> *Cords.*

BOY: 'When I sat down to play the piano everyone laughed at me.'
MOTHER: 'Why?'
BOY: 'Because there wasn't a chair.'

Who writes the music for a castle?
> *Moats art.*

What fills a field with music?
> *Pop corn.*

If you've enjoyed this half as much as I have, then I've enjoyed it twice as much as you.

Crazy Cars

What type of car does a Chinese man drive?
A Rolls Rice.

What kind of car does a lady in pantomime buy?
A dame-ler.

What is big, red and airy?
A red bus with its windows open.

Why is an old car like a baby?
Because it never goes anywhere without a rattle.

What is the difference between a car and a school?
One breaks up and one breaks down.

CAR DEALER: 'This car has had one careful owner.'
BUYER: 'But it's all smashed up.'
CAR DEALER: 'The others weren't so careful.'

Two drivers, old friends, met at the Golden Gates.
FIRST DRIVER: 'What are you doing up here? I didn't
expect to see you for some time.'
SECOND DRIVER: 'I didn't expect to arrive yet, either.
But I was out in the car with my wife and just before we
reached the M5 she said, "Be an angel and let me
drive." Well, here I am.'

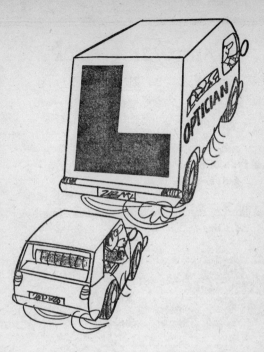

MR BLOGGS: 'Have you managed to start my car yet?'

MECHANIC: 'No, sir, your battery's flat.'

MR BLOGGS: 'Oh dear. What shape should it be?'

Criminal Cracks

Hear about the bank robber who decided to put the money back? He was generous to a vault.

Police notice
Would the motorist who took the first turning off the M1 please put it back.

'Madam, your dog has been chasing a man on a bicycle.'
'Nonsense, officer, my dog can't ride a bicycle.'

What do you call a thief that breaks into a hamburger factory?
>   *A hamburglar.*

What kind of agent does everything twice?
>   *A double agent.*

What do thieves eat for lunch?
>   *Beefburglars.*

POLICEMAN: 'This happens to be a one-way street.'
MOTORIST: 'That's all right, I'm only going one way.'

SHOPKEEPER: 'Inspector, someone has stolen my wig.'
INSPECTOR: 'I'll get my men to comb the area.'

Why is it against the law to whisper?
Because it isn't 'aloud'.

What is the definition of an undercover agent?
A spy in bed.

What kind of spy is always rushing around?
A Russian spy.

Shady? He's the only man I know whose luncheon vouchers bounce.

Newsflash

Last night someone drilled a hole in the fence surrounding a nudist camp. The police are looking into it.

This year's tug-o'-war match between England and France will have to be cancelled unless someone can find a rope 26 miles long.

A villain escaped from prison yesterday by helicopter. The police say they set up road blocks and can't understand how he evaded them.

On Tuesday a man fell into a tank of beer and came to a bitter end.

Today, the Chairman of the Blotto blotting-paper company said he was not going to retire after all because he found his job too absorbing.

Trains out of Paddington Station were running five minutes late yesterday. They will be back to normal tomorrow – running ten minutes late.

Eddie Shoestring, the radio detective, has gone missing. P.C. Blob, Head of New Scotland Yard, said: 'We will soon have this case tied up.'

A lorryload of hair restorer has been spilt on the M1. Police are combing the area.

A baby girl was christened 'Glug-glug' at St Timothy's today. The vicar fell in the font.

Five beds have been stolen from a warehouse. Police say they will spring into action.

A lorry carrying treacle has collided with a car on the M1. Police are advising motorists to stick to their own lanes.

List of Contributors

We have done our best to list everyone's name, and apologize for any that may have been left out. When no address is shown, the jokes came to us with only the sender's name attached.

Jonathon Allsopp, *Tisbury*
Lucy Andrews
J. Askew, *Cheylesmore*
Elizabeth Allen, *Sittingbourne*
Louise Adamson
Clare Ashley, *Marlborough*
Henry Audley-Charles,
 Hurst Green
Paul Arnold, *Canada*
Gideon Amos, *Falmouth*
Marianna Antonis, *London N2*
Hugo Allen, *Richmond*
Tanya Aldridge, *Chesham*
Jill Armstrong, *Lockerbie*
Nadine Arditti
Angie, *St Neots*
Nicola Aldridge, *Aylesbury*
Amir Aujla, *London N20*
Diane Abnett, *Hounslow*
John Astle, *Yatton*
William Adam
Victoria Allen, *Sheffield*
Tim Allman, *Kidderminster*
Sumira Ahmad, *London SW6*
Lizzie Authers, *Truro*
Ruth Allen, *Sittingbourne*
Simon Aldridge, *West Tisbury*

Mandy Atkinson, *Wrelton*
Claire Abbott, *Pickering*
Paul Atkinson, *Pickering*
Tanya Almeida, *London SE21*
Sharon Anglesea, *Colchester*

Liza Boulton, *Rushwick*
Lucy Benson, *London N6*
Emma Jane Barradale, *Walsall*
Stephen Brown, *Stockport*
Jonathon Brooks, *Reading*
David Bailey, *Hythe*
Julie Barnes, *Witham*
Louise Brown, *Rhymney*
Alan Banfield, *Strood*
Liza Burnell, *Kingsnorth*
Anindita Bose
Charlotte Benson,
 London NW5
Janet Bevan-Baker, *Glasgow*
Sarah Bingham, *West
 Bridgford*
Nancy Blabey, *Chislehurst*
Paula Blease, *Shifnal*
Christine Botchway, *Ghana*
Susie Brabner, *Crickhowell*
Magnus Brooke, *Ilkley*

Kate, Martin, Emma and
William Barraball
Christina Brock, *Weston-super-Mare*
Catherine Burns, *Glasgow*
Nancy Tracey-Bower
Anita Bolandage, *Castle Cary*
Alexa Butterworth, *Edinburgh*
Tom Boon, *Penarth*
Richard Barnes
Jenny Bright, *Heswall*
Kate Bendall, *Cambridge*
Andrew Barnes, *St Wenn*
Steven Bowen, *Kidlington*
Nicola Barber
Helen and Carol Bennett,
Sheffield
Iain Frazer Bramhill
Nicholas Barber, *Stock*
Joanna Bracken, *Liverpool*
Wendy Bartlett
Matthew Bell, *Bedford*
Andrew Bayes, *Aylesbury*
David Beech, *Sheffield*
Stephanie Bishop, *Sheffield*
Charmaine Butler, *Aylesbury*
Mark Borrow, *Aylesbury*
Deborah Booth, *Sheffield*
Karen Blakemore, *Sheffield*
Helen Boothroyd, *Huddersfield*
Alison Burton, *Pickering*
Debbie Blakemore, *Sheffield*
Allison Ball, *Sheffield*
Manjit Singh Bhogal,
Birmingham
Emma Buckingham, *Tisbury*
Julie Burdett, *Wallasey*
Emma Bartup
Jeremy and Tania Burchardt
Louise Briffet, *Cumnor Hill,
Oxford*

Tamsin Bradley, *Oxford*
Balmerino Primary School,
Gauldry

Cragside Junior School,
Newcastle-upon-Tyne
Beverley Cull, *Tisbury*
Christopher, *Westisbury*
James Cahill, *Chieveley*
Jill Court, *London N8*
Louisa Cherri, *Hythe*
Stephen Caulton, *Hythe*
Paula Cohen, *Brighton*
Christian Canton,
Rickmansworth
Alexa Crisford, *London NW3*
Clifford Bridge Primary
School, *Binley*
John Chadderton, *Abingdon*
Marcia Chaffey, *Ansty*
Pamela and Sally Chapman,
Nazeing
Hilary Collier, *West Germany*
Helen Cook, *Kirbymoorside*
Sally and Jacob Cutts,
Nuneaton
Alison Clotworthy, *Salisbury*
Stephen Lee Cook, *Swindon*
Louise Clarke, *Wokingham*
Rachael Counihan,
London SW19
Karen Clarke, *Sandbach*
Chris Conroy,
RAF Wildenrath
Martin Claessens, *London N7*
Jayne Colley, *Wribbenhall*
Alison Coray, *Wigston Fields*
Susie Cole, *East Leake*
Caroline Cupitt, *Cambridge*
Irene Chalmers, *Glasgow*
Vaseem Chaudlry, *London
NW10*

Joy Chasmar, *London N14*

N. Chimoindes, *Thetford*

David Cottis, *London SW15*

Andrew Chillingsworth, *Old Duston*

Group V, The Crescent School, *Oxford*

Simon Cooke, *Bebington*

Lucy Collier, *Leighton Buzzard*

J. Cracker, *Hampton*

Jane Cowan, *London E6*

Karen Charman, *Wendover*

Mark Crosse, *Tisbury*

Fiona Campbell, *Pickering*

Sandra Clarke-Irons, *Pickering*

Tanya Cox, *Henley-on-Thames*

Lizzy and Danny Currie, *Oxford*

Elisabeth Courakis, *Headington*

Elizabeth Clift

Astrid Davis, *Maidenhead*

Jane Dreaper, *Winchester*

Lucy Dwyer, *Middleton-on-Sea*

Jimmy Dodman, *Leeds*

Benjamin Dulieu, *Braintree*

Joanna Dixon, *Peterborough*

Charlotte Dodds Price, *London SW20*

Lucinda Denison, *Southampton*

Clinton Dawkins, *Jamaica*

Sara Dhillon, *Weymouth*

Carol Dobson

Joy and Michael Dunn, *Oldham*

Graham Dumper, *Hythe*

Paul Dumper

Neil Dries, *Hythe*

Francesca de Moneva, *Oxton*

Lucy Darwin

Clare Darwin, *London W8*

Neil Dicker, *Tisbury*

Sophie Dobrzynski, *Staleen*

Ghislaine Deeley

Louise Draper, *Exmouth*

Cathy Dodgeon, *St Agnes*

Anthony Dibble

James Davis

Elaine Dunbar, *Newport-on-Tay*

Lee Davey, *Tisbury*

Colin Dunning, *Pickering*

Chrisopher Dixon, *Pickering*

Julia Davies, *Milford Haven*

Robert Davy

Gail Douglas, *Gauldry*

Yvonne Dowkes, *Pickering*

Jane Davidson, *Hastings*

Louise Dodd, *Newnham*

Laura Eaton, *Bristol*

Louisa Edwards, *Woodford Green*

Susan Elsmere, *Basildon*

Rhian Evans, *Anglesey*

Mark Ebner, *Kenton*

Adrian and Jason Emery, *Sandy*

Johanna Ellison, *Stocksfield*

Paula Elliot, *Pickering*

Carolyn Ednie, *Gauldry*

Nicola Edge, *Newton*

Joanna Eastbury, *Yatton*

Susanna Fay, *London N1*

Julie Fulham, *Newcastle-upon-Tyne*

Hilary Forster, *Newcastle-upon-Tyne*
Alison Freemantle, *Tisbury*
Wayne Fox, *Tisbury*
Helen Fox
Joanne Fisher, *Bromley*
Roxanne Fea, *New Zealand*
Andrew Fletcher
Rachael Fernley, *Rickmansworth*
Kelly Anne Fraser, *Gateshead*
Ian Fountain, *Reading*
Rachel Finestein, *Hull*
Jane Fillis, *Norwich*
Sally-Ann Fowler, *Barry*
Justin Foot, *Barrowby*
Lucy Fitzgerald
Carol Fogg, *Kidlington*
Margaret Fluhr, *London SW20*
Tansy Forrest, *West Kirby*
Alfred Fischl, *Glasgow*
Paul Foskett, *Downham*
Chota Fox, *Heworth*
Rachael Fields, *Pickering*
Stuart Fenwick, *Pickering*
Lee Fitton, *Pickering*
Maurice Farrett, *Sheffield*
Christopher Forrie, *Gauldry*

Kim Greengrass, *Birmingham*
Sarah Gudgeon, *Southampton*
Peter and Ruth Grundy, *Wadebridge*
Rachael Green, *Rainhill*
Rachel Goldwyn, *London SW13*
Tracy Gardner, *Hythe*
Lucy Gould, *Winchester*
Lindsay Gowland
Ewen Gibb, *Bearsden*

James Gardner, *March*
Steven Gerrard, *London E17*
Jenny Gerresh, *Bristol*
Cheryl Guidry, *Canada*
Kate Goldfarb, *Countesthorpe*
Rachel Godber, *Copmanthorpe*
Annalise Goodwin, *Hazlemere*
Alison Guy, *Marnhull*
Johanna Gallop, *Yatton*
Samantha Gilmour, *Yatton*
Paul Garner
Amanda Grayson, *Sheffield*
May Gray, *Gauldry*
Adele Gannon, *Burgh-by-Sands*
Nicholas Grayson, *Sheffield*
Stephen Gibson, *Wilton*
Nicky Gully, *Patcham*
Peter Gibson, *Pickering*
Sophia Goldsworthy, *Kennington*
Bridie Griffin
June Gilmour, *Dromore*
Christopher Girling
Ewen Gibb

Michael Holmes, *Countesthorpe*
Jinous Hassanein
Jennifer Hunt, *Storrington*
Anita Harley, *Henlow Camp*
Frances Honir, *Tisbury*
Joanne Hirschmann, *Leeds*
Corrina Harper, *Hythe*
Darran Hazell, *Hythe*
Rebecca Hollingsworth, *Bromley*
Sarah Horton-Jones, *Abergavenny*
Richard Hurford, *Addlestone*

Daniel Harrison, *Kirby Misperton*
Caronline Heape, *Plymouth*
Susan Hawkins, *East Coker*
Yvette Horner, *Isleworth*
Andrew Holmes, *High Wycombe*
Julia Hutchinson, *Baildon*
Jessica Hutton, *Bristol*
Melissa Hutchinson, *Stockton-on-Tees*
Lucie Harris, *Oxford*
Katie Humphries, *Broadstairs*
James Hamilton, *Guilford*
Heath family, *Sheffield*
Jessica Hall–Smith *Liphook*
Penaran Higgs, *Cambridge*
Hythe County Primary School
Wendy Haynes, *Sheffield*
Brett Hollywell, *Oswestry*
Kim Holmes, *Harpenden*
Gareth Hughes, *Edinburgh*
Karen Heckingbottom, *Ipswich*
Sally Hemingray, *Middlesbrough*
Alisbon Herbert, *Swindon*
Catherine Harbert, *Moseley*
Philip Hines, *Eynsham*
Louise Hill, *Bromely*
Guy Hudson, *Limpsfield*
Stuart Hayes, *Hythe*
Claire Hoban, *Liverpool*
Alex Horne
Jayne Hill, *Sheffield*
Elizabeth Harston
Kim Hosmer, *Bromley*
Lorraine Harris, *Bromley*
Beverley Hardy, *Sheffield*
Emily Holland, *Bromley*
Robert Hick, *Bromley*

Tina Holland, *Sheffield*
Caroline Humphries, *Broadstairs*
Rebecca Hills, *Esher*
Nicholas Hardman, *Pickering*
Emma Hack, *Pickering*
Rosalyn Hamilton, *Pickering*
Barry and Caroline Henderson, *Irby*
Rebecca Hardie, *Oxford*
Liza Henton, *Wolvercote*

Jane Irwin, *New Zealand*
Jonathan Inman, *Little Barugh*

Julie Joyce, *Newcastle-upon-Tyne*
Kelly Jones, *Tisbury*
Caroline Jackson, *Alderbury*
Stuart Jones
Emma Jarvis
Karen Jonsen, *Sutton-on-Hull*
Janet Johnson, *Burnham*
Dawn Jarvis, *Canada*
Alison Jones, *Bromley*
David Jones, *Templecombe*
Beverley Johnson, *Banbury*
Colin Jervis, *Dover*
Sarah Jackson, *Windsor*
Abe Juckes, *Mossley Hill*
Keri Jones, *Shiptonthorpe*
Alice Jenkins, *Aylesbury*
Samantha Jones, *Pickering*
Gordon Jackson, *Gauldry*
Marie Jones, *Moreton*

Michael Kilner, *Hatfield*
Karen Kent, *Tisbury*
Sarah Kirby, *Tisbury*
Rebecca Kilgarriff, *London W5*

154

Sandy and Richard King, *Oxford*
Juliet Kavanagh, *London NW1*
Jason King
Debby and Tessa Kirkby, *Bierton*
Suzanne Keys, *Belfast*
Richard Knights
Mary Armstrong Kinmont, *Bishop Auckland*
Ian Kay,
Nicola Kurtz, *Headington*
Harriet Keen, *Oxford*
Matthew Knight, *Aylesbury*
William King, *Pickering*
Nicola Keld, *Pickering*
Claire King, *Pickering*
Fleur Keld, *Pickering*
Lisa Kay, *Pickering*
Andrew Langley, *Trowbridge*
Emma Lane, *York*
Moira Langston, *Bishopbriggs*
Caroline Lovett, *Edmonton*
Alexander Lumby,
Susanna Lent, *Buckhurst Hill*
Robin Lane, *East Grinstead*
Susannah Lloyd, *Kidderminster*
Kristin Lauhn-Jensen, *Canada*
Bruce Logan, *Glasgow*
Tony Lever, *Tisbury*
Jane Liddiard, *Wargrave*
Jane and Thomas Littlewood, *Croydon*
Andrew Langstone, *Solihull*
Clare Lynch, *Skipton*
Alexander Leadbeater, *New Zealand*
Rebecca Lawrence, *London W12*

Beverley Lack, *Pickering*
William and Caroline Lee, *Wirral*
Sarah Lund, *Biggleswade*

Vicky Marsh, *Atherton*
Sarah Mayes, *Bournemouth*
Kevin Moor, *Newcastle*
Jane Middlemiss, *Newcastle*
Suzanne Mogford, *Tisbury*
Sarah Marshall, *Tisbury*
Ashley Maddison, *Tatsfield*
Lucy Marshall, *Tisbury*
Charlotte McLeod
Sophie Marsh
Hannah Moore, *Gravesend*
Alison Mapp, *Bridgnorth*
Alan McCulloch, *Rugby*
Stephen McHarg, *Whitehaven*
Sarah Moore
Anna Murphy, *Yatton*
Sophie Malik, *Tunbridge Wells*
Marina Miller, *Ashtead*
Nicola Jane Moore, *Launceston*
Michael Martin, *Dunfermline*
Katie Myers, *London SW20*
Catherine Marcer, *Southampton*
Lara Mathias, *York*
Matthew Marchant, *Exeter*
Andrew Morrison, *London N10*
Elizabeth Marsh, *Old Bolingbroke*
Sarah McBride, *U.S.A.*
Victoria Melhereth, *Fareham*
Jennifer Moss, *Leek*
Adrian Moore, *Orpington*
Jonathan Mott, *Loughborough*
Matthew Marsden, *Riddlington*
Amos Miller, *Bristol*

Josephine Mole, *Rotherham*
Raechel Murray, *Woking*
Rebecca Morris, *Stourbridge*
Lucy and Peter Macmillan
Catherine Monk, *Toddington*
Darren Miller, *Dovercourt*
Sheelagh Matthers, *Bangor*
Donna McGuire, *Glasgow*
Rebecca Mead
Nigel Morris, *Clywd*
Miles Mercer, *Wirral*
Phillipa Milner
Heather MacKenzie, *Gauldry*
Nick Marchant, *Exeter*
Marguerite Mellers, *Great Barugh*
Jonathan Martindale, *Pickering*
Sarah Mansfield, *Wilton*
Neil Matthew, *Gauldry*
Lori McLeon, *Healing*
Andrew Moorby, *Bebington*
Nicola Montgomery, *Brighton*
Margaret Hardy Youth Club
Geeta Mayor, *Seven Kings*
Cardine Messenger, *Boar's Hill*
Kevin Mills *London SW1*
Middleton Road County Junior School, *Pickering*

Kim Nissan, *London SW3*
Deborah Nash, *Bexhill-on-Sea*
Anaelechi Nnadi, *London W1*
Katherine and Danielle Nurse, *Harrow*
Alison Naylor, *Lincoln*
K. Noseda, *Little Cambridge*
Sushila and Peter Newell, *London E1*

Lyndy Northover, *Reading*
Rebecca Neale, *Brislington*
Christopher North, *Yatton*
Susan Norman, *Bromley*
Lucy and Annabel Newnam, *Thames Ditton*
John Newman, *Pickering*
Kathrine Newitt, *Newport-on-Tay*

Onyeaso Family
Jennifer Orpwood, *Wantage*
Kirsten Orr, *Greenock*
Willow Ovenden, *Harrogate*
Fiona and Linda Oliphant, *Lockerbie*
James Osborne, *London SE10*
Jonathan Ollier, *Oswestry*
Sian O'Neill, *London NW1*
Vickie Orton, *Helensburgh*

Graham Pointe
Franca Pantrini, *Harborne*
Elizabeth Palmer, *Surbiton*
Susan Paddock, *Petersfield*
Thomas Pattison, *Hull*
Marcus Pailing, *Orpington*
Sharon Parkes, *Reading*
Mrs M. Parrott, *Newton Abbott*
Eleanor Parry
Elaine Powell, *London SW11*
Clive Pudd, *Towcester*
Sigrid Pettenburg, *South-West Africa*
Margaret Porthouse, *Cleadon*
Jane Packwood, *Charlestown*
Diane Powell, *Churchstoke*
Emily Payze
Amy Prior
Karen Pagett, *Kings Heath*
Zoe Phillips

Caroline Pailing, *Orpington*
Candida and Emma Pierce
David Plumbley, *Hoole*
Michele Perry, *Yatton*
Andrew Powell
Nicola Parker, *Bromley*
Scott Pryde, *Dundee*
Geraldine Pool, *Pickering*
Louise and Richard Pateman, *Pickering*
Philip Pape, *Pickering*
Kathleen Pirie, *Newport-on-Tay*
Sarah Peaks, *Erith*

Sarah and Jane Quarmby, *London SE23*
W. Quest, *Yatton*

Simon Rawlinson
Stephen Rodgers, *Leighton Buzzard*
Darren Rochford, *Kidlington*
Angela Renshaw
Polly Richards, *London W11*
Emma Rae, *Edinburgh*
Reglan Junior School, *Bromley*
Caroline Rowe, *London E4*
Kathyrn Robinson, *Bishop Auckland*
Victoria Richardson, *London NW1*
Sarah Rudman
Matthew Robson, *Barton-on-Humber*
Gail Rozario, *Kenton*
Rosemary Nepean, *Canada*
Miss S. Rudman, *Bradford on Avon*
Helen and Joanna Richardson, *Hong Kong*

Melanie Randall, *Enfield*
Victoria Richards
Caroline Rosen, *London E11*
Dawn Rutherford, *Haughley*
Tabitha Rubbra, *Speen*
Daniel Richards, *Barry*
Candy Roberts-Sencicle, *Caliane*
Bryan Roberts
Ann Robinson, *Didsbury*
Jennifer Rodger, *London W1*
Jake Roe, *London SE12*
Emma Rees, *Oxwich*
Justin Rees, *Richmond*
Helen Rees, *Sheffield*
Mark Reeves, *Pickering*
Sara Redfearn, *Sheffield*
Keith Russell, *Gauldry*
Jane Rudgard, *Newton-upon-Rawcliffe*
Vicki Rolf, *Patcham*
Elizabeth Roberts, *Swallowcliffe*
Philip Ridout, *Tisbury*

Claire Shaw, *Cambridge*
Leza Sheppard, *Tisbury*
Amanda Scott, *Swallowcliffe*
Terri Sanger, *Tisbury*
Jacqueline Smoker, *Tisbury*
Andrea Sapscord, *London W13*
Angela Stacey, *Headington*
John Searle, *Adderbury*
Lisa Shipway, *Hythe*
Bryony Smith, *Sketty*
Barry Spenceley, *Wantage*
Hannah Smith, *Hythe*
Duncan Sanders
Elizabeth Sturch
Alka Sood, *Nottingham*
Jessica Scanlon, *Oxford*
Trevor Stack

Elizabeth Sisson, *Hythe*
Nicola Smith, *Warminster*
Miss J. Swaffield, *Uxbridge*
Michael Stone, *Ongar*
Catherine Sayer, *Thurcaston*
Sophia, *Peacehaven*
Mark Smith
Dawn Simpson
Elizabeth Shuter, *Hethersett*
Howard Smith, *Romford*
Sally Scott, *St Albans*
Matthew Shaddick, *London
SE26*
Juliet Starr, *London NW8*
Amanda Standing, *Sunningdale*
Sarah Sturch, *Northwood Hills*
Zella Swift, *Bury St Edmunds*
Sian Sinderby, *Cwmbran*
Adrian Sanger, *Ringwood*
Sarah Shaw, *Bromsgrove*
Kate, Clare, Lucy and
Rebecca Southwood,
Boxmoor
Gurjeet Singh, *Birmingham*
Kimberley Small, *Petersfield*
Alexia Short, *Bath*
Kathy Shortle, *Witney*
Rowena Sweatman, *Lightwater*
C. Severn, *Allertree*
Nicholas Spong, *London N4*
Neil Sladen, *Penwortham*
Jason Seaward, *Little Bookham*
Sharon Spittals, *Aylesbury*
Michael Stevens, *Yatton*
D. Syer, *Durham*
Colin Smith, *Gauldry*
Marc Sherriff, *Gauldry*
Kay Showell, *Gauldry*
Mandy Strange, *Tisbury*
Adrian Sherwen, *Larkhall*
Paul and Karen Shanks,
Pickering

Andrew Stanton, *Pickering*
David Swithenbank,
Pickering
Julie Sumner, *Pickering*
Lisa Simpson, *Pickering*
Louise Skelly, *Pickering*
Peter Stanton, *Brighton*
Patrick Sharkey, *Enfield*
Petroc Trelawny, *Helston*
Simon Topping, *Newcastle-
upon-Tyne*
Menaka Thiru, *Cambridge*
Gabriel Taranowski,
London SW14
Alex Taylor, *London NW2*
Vincent Taylor, *Littlemore*
Akihito Takeuchi, *Japan*
Dawn Thompson, *Dover*
Derry Thorburn, *London N20*
Elisabeth Telcs, *London N3*
Sarah Templey, *Brookmans
Park*
Nigel Thomas, *Oswestry*
Hilary Teague, *New Malden*
Victoria Tonge, *Langnor*
Sonya Thomas, *Crowthorne*
Josephine Tulloh, *Marlborough*
Ian Talbot, *Abingdon*
Joanna Turner, *Freshwater
Bay*
Peter Tristram, *Stourbridge*
Karl Thurgood, *Pinner*
Ian Thomson
Gillian Turnbull, *Pickering*
Stuart Tyler, *Cardiff*

Stephanie Vinson, *Kernsdale*
Allison Vasey, *Newcastle-
upon-Tyne*
Diccon Vokins, *Bristol*
Victoria Vaughan

Joanna Wood, *Salisbury*
Elizabeth Watts, *Dover*
Lisa Wainer
S. Wills
Susan White, *Worksop*
Michelle Woods, *Tisbury*
Stephen Wilkinson,
 Tuckingmill
J. P. Wilson, *Sherwood*
David Woodhead, *Hythe*
Karen Williams, *Hythe*
Alan White, *Tisbury*
Ian Wyatt, *Adderbury*
Stephen Woolnough, *Hoole*
Mrs P. Whetton,
 Mansfield
Eloise Wylie, *Crewe*
Louise Webb, *Kenilworth*
Tessa Watson, *Upminster*
Terry Williams, *Newent*
Sian Williams, *Edinburgh*
Samantha Wade, *Brough*
Lloyd Webb, *Paddock Wood*
Richard Weller, *Reading*
Anthony Wilson, *Towcester*
Simon Wright, *Northfleet*
Hannah Wiskin, *Leek*
Kelly Winward, *Reigate*
Julianne Waugh, *Donaghadee*
Phil Weiss, *London W11*
Tim Wootton, *Tunbridge Wells*
Thomas and Zander Watt
Alison Wakely, *Honiton*
Sally Watson, *Upminster*
Oliver White, *St Ives*
Fiona Wilson, *Bearsden*
Alison Waters, *Ludlow*
Philippa Welch, *Rotherham*
Stephen Whittle, *Stannington*
Georgina Whittaker,
 Bromley
Jane Williams, *Wells*

Jane Ward, *Spalding*
Andrew Williams,
 Llandrindod Wells
Matilda Webb, *Cropton*
Jane Whitton, *Sheffield*
Sarah Wyte, *Caythorpe*
William Wastie, *Eastbourne*
Hedley Whewell, *Kendal*
Rebekah Wood, *Philippines*
Matthew Wheeler, *Aylesbury*
Peter Williams, *Yatton*
Joanne Whatley, *Downham*
Andrew Warren, *Sheffield*
Angela Wagland, *Sheffield*
Michelle Walkerdine,
 Sheffield
Carol and Ann Weigel,
 Gauldry
Mia Wood, *London NW3*
Clare Wilson
Andrea Welburn, *Kirby
 Misperton*
Theresa Watson, *Pickering*
Sharron Walker, *Pickering*
Sara Webster, *Pickering*
Andrea Woodward, *Pickering*
Tracey Whitehead, *Pickering*
Jason Williams, *Tisbury*
Stuart Wood, *Pickering*
Graham Worton, *Wolvercote*
Karen Worton, *Wolvercote*

Rachel Yapp
Gareth Young, *Basingstoke*
Stuart and Angela Young,
 Carlisle
Samantha Young, *London E4*
Yatton Junior School,
 Bristol
Michael Yates, *Sheffield*

Richard Stanley (picture opposite) lives in the village of Wolvercote, near Oxford. A journalist and broadcaster, he has worked for both the BBC and ITV and as a freelance writer for many major national newspapers and magazines. He has also worked for two large charity organizations: Oxfam and The International Year of the Child, for which he was the UK Appeals Director. Whilst working for these organizations, he was involved in setting up the publication of two Puffin books for charity, both of which were tremendously successful: *The Crack-a-Joke Book* and *I Like This Poem*. His work in the charity field continues, for he is now Chief Executive of Radio Lollipop, Britain's first national hospital radio service for children.

Together with his two young sons, Giles and Matthew, he greatly enjoys reading and collecting the 'awful' jokes that children from all over the world send in to him. If you would like to write to Richard about this book and send in your favourite terrible jokes, rhymes, recipes and insults for a possible future book, send them to *Richard Stanley, c/o Puffin Books, 536 King's Road, London SW10*.